# Legally Black

## From Street Kid To Law Student

Ralston D. Jarrett, J.D.

Editor: Kayla E. Jarrett & Roxanne N. Jarrett

Creative Direction, Cover & Interior Design- Grace Media & Consulting LLC (Alexis M. Jarrett)

**ISBN-13: 978-0-692-10052-3**

DEDICATION

This book is dedicated to my mother, Reebe, and
my father, Ralston Sr. It is additionally dedicated to my sister, Roxanne, my niece, Lauren,
and the rest of the extended Jarrett/Taylor family.
Special thanks to Faulkner University's Jones School of Law for allowing a young kid from
Columbus, Georgia to make something out of himself.

- Ralston Darnell Jarrett

# CONTENTS

# PROLOGUE

I will never forget the day I thought I had been shot. It was a Friday night in my sophomore year of college. While in college I would study hard and go to classes Monday through Thursday, but Friday nights were usually reserved for partying. This was a Friday night I would never forget.

During my second year of college my friends asked me to attend a party. I got dressed and they came to pick me up. The night was nothing out of the ordinary; my friends and I went to the party trying to pick up girls. That is how it usually went, we would see women dancing and go up behind them to see if one would dance along with us. This was an indirect way of asking them to dance. Sometimes they would dance with us and sometimes we would get turned down. It was all in good fun, if you get her to dance, you look over and smile at your friends like "yeah, I'm the man." And if she rejected you, then your friends would look over and laugh as you awkwardly walked away. This was our thing that we would often do, go to the college parties and have a competition to see who would be able to get the most dances and phone numbers.

At about 2:00am the lights came on and it was time to go. I was standing outside talking with my friends, waiting on this girl I had danced with earlier that night to walk out so I could ask for her number. While talking to my friends I was suddenly attacked a cold sucker punch to my right eye. While I did not fall, the unexpected punch by the unknown assailant put me in a daze. After the sneak attack, the assailant took off running. I was too dazed to give chase and he disappeared in the crowd of the already scattering party goers.

Partially blind, I gained my composure. I heard the crowd dispersing and I was looking for my friends. Surely, they had caught the guy who hit me and were beating him to smithereens. I looked to my left, nothing. I looked over to my right, nothing. I looked up and they were both by the car. Now I am mad. I started to make my way toward them, and guess who was there? The guy who hit me along with two other guys beside him. I glanced at him to see who in the heck just hit me in my face for no apparent reason. I had never seen the guy before in my life. He was a slim guy about my size, twists in his hair and he looked kind of dusty and poor. My instincts were saying attack him, but was three of them and I was by myself. The guy next to him slightly bigger than the both of us asked me to take off my chain I was wearing. I stared him down.

He asked again, "Let me get that chain up off ya?"

"Fuck you nigga!" I yelled.

The guys were not alone and their friends, after hearing all the commotion, quickly joined alongside them. So now instead of just three, it's about eight of them. Still not wanting to back down I said, "Fuck all y'all niggas, I'm from the East!"

I was talking tough, but I was really looking for a place to run. They were all in front of me. I glanced behind me and saw nothing but some bushes and a gate. I did the only thing I could do -- got into a fighting stance.

Out of nowhere an old high school named Wade intervened. Wade was a bigger guy, a former collegiate football player who knew me and knew them as well. Wade stepped in and stopped me from getting jumped.

He yelled at them all, "He cool folk! Ralston go head man!"

I walked to the car pissed at the friends who had left me alone. I instantly get in the car and I guess my body language said *let's go I don't have anything to say to you all.* My friend, the driver, knowing me to not be a trouble maker, got out of the car and proceeded to ask the guys, "Why are y'all trying to jump Ralston?"

They replied with something rude and he retreated back into the car. The next thing you know they're surrounding us. I saw Wade and he was trying to hold them back, but there were just too many of them. My friend driving rammed the car in gear while they kicked, punched, spat and scratched at the car. The next thing you know, I heard the loudest noise ever. Boom! The passenger side glass shattered everywhere. I instantly grabbed my neck because I was in immerse pain and bleeding heavily. My friend floored it and we went a few blocks over before we could stop to check on me. My neck was bleeding and I was feeling weak. I looked down at the floorboard and there was a broken beer bottle. The loud boom (while at the time I could have sworn was a bullet from the loud bang it made upon impact) was simply a beer bottle one of the attackers had thrown through the window. The flying shattered glass pierced my neck and caused serve damage.

The next day, after word had gotten back around about the incident, a group of my friends, probably angrier than I was, gathered at my house to check on me. They made sure I was okay and told me to get ready for next Friday.

The next Friday night three cars showed up to my house with some of my closest friends looking for retaliation. I was cool about the situation after a week had passed, but my friends -- not so much. The driver was mad because they had destroyed his car, causing hundreds of dollars' worth of damage. I was okay though, I still had my chain and a new found respect in my neighborhood once the word got back around that I had not given the chain up and squared up (slang for got in a fighting stance) with 8 to 10 guys that were twice my size.

I am not sure why but my friends were always like my big brothers, and they did not like anyone messing with me. Not wanting to seem like a punk, I got into one of the cars. I will never forget when one of my best friends, ( Whiteboy Chris, who was one of the only white guys in our neighborhood) showed me his pistol. With this being my first time seeing a gun, I smiled at him but was horrified inside. I mean, I had seen guns in movies, but never a real one. During the car ride down to the party spot where the incident occurred I was silent, but they were talking about how they wanted something to happen tonight.

"They think they can jump on Ralston and get away with it? I got something for them," my friends were livid and sought revenge.

I was there physically, but mentally my mind was rushing 100 miles per hour.

On one hand, I did want to fight the guy who sucker punched me. On the other hand, I did not want any of the guys who attacked me to get shot, or anything to happen to any of my friends all of whom I had grown up with. But they were down to protect me and even shoot someone if necessary for my beef, what was I to do? Say no? I was scared, but I did not let it show. We got down to the spot and

everyone walked to the building. It was about 10 to 12 of us. The party was dead, so we just sat and waited outside laughing and I was praying to God in the back of my head that these guys do not show up.
Every time a car pulled up, my friends would ask, "Ralston is that them?" Thankfully, they never showed, we ended up leaving about 1:30am and went to a local all-night diner to eat. I bragged and boasted to my peers about what I would have done if those guys would've have shown up that night, but deep down inside I was glad they had not come.

This event was a turning point in my life. While the attempted robbers tried to rob me of a necklace, they did not realize they had taken something way more valuable from me, my innocence. Up until that point I had no reason to fear anything, I honestly thought that no one would hurt me without adequate provocation.

Immediately after the robbery attempt, I purchased my first gun, an all-black 9 millimeter. I did not get it for revenge or with the intent to hurt anyone, but simply for my protection. I never wanted to feel that helpless in a situation ever again. While I may look and even act like a normal person, I am not (which I will elaborate on more throughout the book). There is much more to me than what meets the eye.

Being a man is not easy, we are driven by egos that can get too big at times and a heart full of pride which can be one's down fall. Looking back at it now, should we have gone back to the same exact spot I had almost gotten robbed the week before with weapons looking for trouble? No, of course not. Should I have just given the chain up that night? I am not sure. I ask myself that question all the time. My ego was too big at the time to let another man say he had taken something from me and my pride simply would not allow it.

My journey to get to law school and to stay there was a roller coaster ride, filled with many ups and downs. There is no handbook for life or for law school. When there is no handbook, we tend to go with the flow (which can be a good thing or a bad thing). We all know what happens when boats go with the flow of the sea and have no real destination. The person or the boat may luck up; but both are more likely to crash. The same thing happens to people who go with the flow of life with no handbook or navigation. They may luck up, but they are most likely destined to crash as well.

This book was intended to suffice as a handbook for our generation of upcoming law students, college students, medical students and anyone else who is willing to listen.

Our parents, teachers and even our coaches try to tell about life, but we disregard them. However, the values they instill in us never go away. Sometimes it is easy to allow the words they say to go in one ear and out the other. Hopefully, my story will stick in the minds of young people for years and years to come. This is my journey to get here (law school), and I do not expect everyone to understand or even agree with my way of thinking and some of the decisions I have made while navigating through life. I hope everyone will enjoy the book and find inspiration from a young Black male who came from humble beginnings and jumped on to the path to become a law student and future attorney despite the many obstacles I have encountered.

# PART I

# Chapter 1

## THE LAST ASSIGNMENT

This is my last semester of law school, I am sitting down in my bar preparation course on a Wednesday afternoon around 12:50pm. I must have started daydreaming while my boy Mike was asking the professor some complex question that went over the heads of the rest of the class, including myself. I look around the classroom and realize its only eight weeks until we all graduate from law school. To the right of me sits Tiffany, or Tiff, as I always call her who ended up becoming my law school best friend. To the left of me sits Devon my homeboy from Auburn, Alabama who is a Sigma and will inform you of his Greek affiliation every chance he has. Beside him Reggie, Army Veteran turned law student. In front of me my main man, Aaron, ex-football star turned law student. Next to him, Caleb, the top law student in our graduating class. On the other side of the classroom sat Haley and Audrey, vividly taking notes while the professor is talking to Mike.

Sometimes it is hard for me to take in that these guys are going to be leaders around our country very soon and I was among this group. While I had struggled with them, argued with them, studied with them and partied with them since our very first days together at law school, it was still hard to believe sometimes. While just a few years ago, these people were complete strangers, but over the last three years we had all developed a special and unique bond. I was really about to graduate from law school and I could not believe it. Good things like this just did not happen to people like me. The professor looks my way and I snap out of my daze and slap a few of the keys on my computer in front of me just to make it look like I was taking notes, when I really had not heard a word she said.

She looks right above my head at the wall clock and says, "Alright class, see you all next week. Make sure you do those evidence questions and complete essay two before next Wednesday."

I stand up and stretch out. I had been sitting for 90 minutes and my butt was numb; fold my laptop and place it in my bag. I look over at Tiff, Reggie and Devon and ask, "What y'all about to do? I'm hungry as a fool!"

They all laugh and Reggie responds, "I don't know man, I'm hungry too though. Ya'll want to get something to eat?"

"Man I would, got to head over to work though," Devon replies.

Tiff looks at us and shrugs. "Yeah we can."

"Cool. Let's hit up that new Jamaican restaurant downtown, they just opened up. I want some jerk chicken," I reply.

We head out the classroom and are walking toward the elevator while engaged in conversation. We are right in front of the elevator when I hear a soft voice call my name.

"Mr. Jarrett? Mr. Jarrett?" I turn around and it is Dean Rivera, she is the school's Academic Dean.

I quickly turn on my professional mannerism, "Hello Dean Rivera."

She looks at me and smiles "Hello, Mr. Jarrett. Do you have a minute? Can you come to my office? I would like to speak with you."

"Yes, sure that's no problem," I respond.

I turn around to Tiff and Reggie who are holding the elevator open for me with looks of concern on their faces.

"Go ahead y'all. I'll catch up with you guys later."

"Okay Ralston."

The elevator closes and I proceed to follow Dean Rivera to the Dean's Suite where her office is located (which at the time seemed like the longest walk ever). In my head, I am thinking *what could she possibly want?* I had not done anything wrong.

"Have a seat Mr. Jarrett." She proceeds to close the door behind her. "Mr. Jarrett, I wanted to talk to you about graduation."

I lose it and start freaking out, my mouth moving a mile a minute. "What! What happened? I ordered that cap and gown over a month ago! They didn't place the order in time, huh? Man. I have to graduate I have family coming from all over the country. I made my graduation announcements already. They shipped yesterday. Dean Rivera, I paid $90 for those announcements, they have my picture on them and they are non-refundable. Oh my gosh, what am I going to tell my mom? She already bought her dress to wear to my graduation."

She looks at me and stands up to calm me down. "No, Mr. Jarrett it's not what you think, you are still graduating."

I look up at her relieved and smile like *Dean Rivera you scared me for a second there.*

"Sorry Mr. Jarrett, but let me get straight to the point. It does look as if you are two credits short from the required 88 needed to graduate. The good news is that it was not your fault and it seems to be a computer error on our part."

I chime in, "Oh, so I'm okay then?"

"Yes, you will graduate on time, but to make up for the two credits you are missing you will need to earn those."

I look at her in confusion. "Dean Rivera, it's eight weeks before graduation, how do you expect me to get two credits when all the classes are full and have already began?"

"That's what I wanted to talk to you about. I have talked to the rest of the Deans in the school and we all agree that you are an exceptional student who has really had an impact on our school. We have given you a choice. You may either pick up an extra class, although they are full we can make an opening if needed, or you can write a legal memorandum on a topic of my choosing."

I look up into the air in contemplation. "Yeah, umm… I will take the legal memorandum."

She smiles. "Excellent Mr. Jarrett, I will send you the task instructions before the end of the week.

I get up and shake her hand. "Okay and thank you again, sorry for the rambling I did earlier, I kind of panicked."

"Totally understandable," she laughs. "You have a good day" I turn around and walk swiftly out of her office.

**Faulkner University: Jones School of Law**

5500 Atlanta Highway Montgomery, AL 36117
(334) 555-5555

MEMORANDUM

To: Ralston Jarrett
From: Dean Rivera
Date: March 8, 2017
Re: Memo for Incoming Students Class of 2020

One of our longtime traditions here at Faulkner University is to provide an equal opportunity for all students to learn. Over the last five years Jones School of law has become one of the most diverse law schools in the country. To keep this tradition going the Deans and I have all agreed that you are one of the most promising students on the campus and want to hear about your overall experience at Faulkner. As the Academic Dean, I would also like to know more about who Ralston Jarrett is. I am currently working on the admissions for the incoming class of 2020. There are currently two students in particular that I would like your input on how to properly inform them about our law school in order to see if this is the right place for them. I have conducted their phone interviews and have attached the transcripts to this email. Please draft a memorandum for me as if you were personally advising the potential students including but not limited to the following:

I. What was your motivation for coming to law school?
II. What does it take to be a successful law student?
III. Any other relevant information you think would help in their law school journey.

A separate fact section is not necessary. However, you should incorporate relevant facts of your life to analyze and address the students concerns they expressed in the transcripts attached. Be sure to make the memo clear and concise, but also informative. Citing legal authority will not be necessary as the memorandum will be for my personal use and may even be sent to the students who will not understand legal cites. Let me know if you have any further questions. Good luck on your final memorandum.

**TRANSCRIPT OF STUDENT INTERVIEW:**

**Jordan McKinney**

**February 13, 2017**

**Dean Rivera:** Hello, this is Jennifer Rivera from Faulkner Law also known as Thomas Goode Jones School of Law. Is Jordan available?

**Jordan McKinney:** Hi, this is Jordan speaking.

**Dean Rivera:** Hello Jordan, do you have a minute to talk? We have received your law school application and I would like to conduct a telephone interview with you as part of the first step towards processing your application.

**Jordan McKinney**: Oh, yes. That is fine. Excuse me if I sound nervous I was not expecting this.

**Dean Rivera**: Oh, you are fine. It will just be a few questions and sorry if I interrupted anything. We usually like to conduct these phone interviews spontaneously so people will not have time to rehearse. We here at Faulkner like to get a feel for the real person to see if they would be a good fit for our school.

**Jordan McKinney**: No, you were not interrupting anything I was actually just getting in from the store.

**Dean Rivera**: Okay, great well let me know when you are ready and we can get started. Just a reminder that this does not mean you have been accepted, nor does it mean that you are going to get accepted. The phone interview just gives us a glimpse of who you are and it is recorded for our record keeping.

**Jordan McKinney**: Okay, I understand. Well I am ready to start whenever you are.

**Dean Rivera**: Please state your name, race, sex and age. If you would wish to not have this disclosed, please say next question.

**Jordan McKinney:** My name is Jordan Rebecca McKinney**,** and I am a 24-year-old, white, female.

**Dean Rivera:** Where do you currently live? How long have you lived there? And have you ever been to Alabama?

**Jordan McKinney:** I currently live in Woodbury, Minnesota. I have lived here for 14 years and no I have never been to Alabama before. But I have always wanted to visit. I am a big Alabama football fan. My family and I get together to watch them play every time they have a big game on television.

**Dean Rivera:** What is your current marital status?

**Jordan McKinney:** I am engaged, my boyfriend of 3 years proposed to me last New Year's Eve. We plan to get married before I leave for school and he is going to come with me to law school.

**Dean Rivera:** Is anyone in your family a lawyer?

**Jordan McKinney:** No, I would be the first one in my family to be a lawyer. My older brother is a doctor in St. Paul, Minnesota. He went to medical school, but I will be the first one in our family to attend law school.

**Dean Rivera:** Why do you want to come to law school?

**Jordan McKinney:** I want to make a difference in the world.

**Dean Rivera:** What type of law do you want to practice?

**Jordan McKinney:** I want to practice family law. You see, at the age of 7 my mother died from Breast Cancer. I lived with my father who one day gave my older brother and I to his sister in Woodbury and said he would come back for us, but he never did. My aunt and her husband took us in and treated us well. So well that they ended up adopting my brother and me. So, that's what I want to do. I want to be an adoption lawyer to help with the process of adopting children in need.

**Dean Rivera:** What type of student would you say you were?

**Jordan McKinney:** I am a great student. I graduated at the top of my class at my college. I participate in many on campus activities. And I volunteer to feed the homeless two times a week.

**Dean Rivera:** What would you be able to contribute to Jones School of Law if admitted?

**Jordan McKinney:** I think my personality will be my contribution. On the brochure, Jones looks as if it is a great school in a small town. Being from

Woodbury, Minnesota which is a very small town I think I will be able to bring my vibrant personality to the campus and will not feel out of place in Montgomery, as I might in a bigger city with a bigger school.

**Dean Rivera:** Is there anything else you would like the admissions staff to know about you?

**Jordan McKinney:** Yes, I just want them to know that they will not be disappointed if they let me into Jones School of Law. I have dreamed about coming to law school for as long as I can remember, and if they decide to give me the opportunity to attend, I promise to work hard and to persevere to make this dream a reality.

**Dean Rivera:** Anything else? Any concerns you wanted to address?

**Jordan McKinney:** Yes, I was a little concerned about the cost of law school. I come from a middle-class home and I was seeing if it would be able to afford it. Then, I was just asking myself would it be worth the cost in the long run.

**Dean Rivera:** That is understandable. Keep in mind that if you are accepted we offer a variety of scholarships and have paid student job opportunities available. As for the second concern, I think that is more of a subjective question I can get a few students to answer that if you would like.

**Jordan McKinney:** Yes, that would be lovely. I would really appreciate that.

**Dean Rivera:** No problem. Well Jordan that wraps it up. You did great! We will add this to your application folder, review it and you can expect to hear from Jones within 4-6 weeks. We will mail a letter and send an email regarding our decision on your acceptance. Thank you.

**Jordan McKinney:** No problem Mrs. Rivera, I appreciate Faulkner for even considering me for their school. Thank You.

**Dean Rivera**: Thank you Ms. McKinney. The best of luck to you. Good bye.

**Jordan McKinney**: Thank You. Goodbye.

**TRANSCRIPT OF STUDENT INTERVIEW:**

**Nicholas Brooks**

**February 21, 2017**

**Dean Rivera:** Hello, this is Jennifer Rivera from Faulkner Law also known as Thomas Goode Jones School of Law. Is Nicholas Brooks available?

**Nicholas Brooks:** Hello this is Nicholas Brooks. Who am I speaking with again?

**Dean Rivera**: This is Jennifer Rivera I am a part of the Admissions Staff at Jones School of Law here in Montgomery, Alabama.

**Nicholas Brooks:** Oh yes, how are you? Excuse me I did not recognize the number.

**Dean Rivera:** I'm doing well Nicholas thank you for asking. If you have a few minutes I would like to ask you a few questions concerning your law school application.

**Nicholas Brooks:** Okay, that sounds great.

**Dean Rivera**: Okay, great well let's get started. Just a reminder Nicholas that this does not mean you have been accepted, nor does it mean that you are going to get accepted. The phone interview just gives us a glimpse of who you are and it is recorded for our record keeping.

**Nicholas Brooks:** Yes, I understand. I am ready.

**Dean Rivera**: Please state your name, race, sex and age. If you'd wish to not have this disclosed, please say next question.

**Nicholas Brooks:** My name is Nicholas Brooks, I am a 26-year-old, African American, male.

**Dean Rivera:** Where do you currently live? How long have you lived there? And have you ever been to Alabama?

**Nicholas Brooks:** I reside in Chicago, Illinois. I have lived here for 26 years and yes, I have been to Alabama one time. I came to visit some family in Birmingham when I was about 18.

**Dean Rivera:** How did you like Birmingham?

**Nicholas Brooks:** Birmingham was nice. I was only there for three months. When I was 18 my mom sent me down there for the summer to keep me from getting into trouble here in Chicago. It was nice. The people were very friendly, but country.

**Dean Rivera:** Yes, Birmingham is very nice. It is about an hour from the law school. It is good to see you have experienced what we call southern hospitality.

**Nicholas Brooks:** Hospitality is the correct word. It was really a different world down there. Everyone was very nice. In Chicago, the people here are not as polite.

**Dean Rivera:** How is life in Chicago? Are you in the inner city or more in the outskirts of the city?

**Nicholas Brooks:** I am in the inner city of Chicago. South Side to be exact. It is okay here. But it is really easy to get into trouble here. The gangs in Chicago are very prevalent. Luckily, I always used school as an escape to get away from the street gang lifestyle.

**Dean Rivera:** What is your current marital status?

**Nicholas Brooks:** I am single. I do have a 4-year-old daughter named Raquel. Her mother and I were engaged, but things did not work out between us.

**Dean Rivera:** Do you have anyone in your family who is a lawyer? Other Professions?

**Nicholas Brooks:** No, unfortunately the majority of my family are gang members. I am the first one to even go to college. Let alone law school.

**Dean Rivera:** Why do you want to come to law school?

**Nicholas Brooks:** Back in 2010. My brother was arrested here in Chicago after a local playground was shot up and a 3-year-old girl was killed. The police who were anxious to make an arrest, rounded up every black male in the vicinity which my brother so happened to be in. They gathered them together for a lineup and a witness pointed out my brother as one of the accomplices and they arrested him. Meanwhile, the real shooter was not identified in the lineup. My family was devastated. We had no money to pay his bail, we could not afford a lawyer. We talked to him daily and did everything we could to get him to tell the police who the real shooter was. We grew up with the guy so my brother would not tell. So, after 180 days sitting in jail for something he did not do the prosecution called his court appointed defense attorney and made him a deal. Plead guilty to a lesser charge and get a 5-year sentence with 6 months to serve, and walk out today for time served and the rest on a probationary supervision or go to trial for an accomplice of murder. My brother took the plea. He was tired physically and mentally. Just a case of being at the wrong place at the wrong time, with the wrong crowd. What's worse than this is while my brother did hang out with gang bangers before he went to jail, he was not in a gang, he came home worse than when he went in. Jail changed him tremendously. So, that is one of the reasons I want to come to law school. I feel as if my brother would have had me as his lawyer he would not have went down the wrong path. I just want to save other males from the same cycle by making sure they get adequate legal representation.

**Dean Rivera:** Wow, well good for you. What type of law do you want to practice? Criminal?

**Nicholas Brooks:** Yes, I would love to learn as much as I can about criminal law to become a criminal defense attorney one day.

**Dean Rivera:** What type of student would you say you were?

**Nicholas Brooks:** I am a very visual learner. Teachers at my school were always impressed on how I could remember everything they wrote on the board. But, overall, I think I am a great student, I always do my best and give all my assignments my best effort.

**Dean Rivera:** What would you be able to contribute to Jones School of law if you were admitted?

**Nicholas Brooks:** That is a good question. I am not sure exactly. Diversity I guess.

**Dean Rivera:** Is there anything else you would like the admissions staff to know about you?

**Nicholas Brooks:** Yes, I have been diagnosed with Sickle Cell Anemia. While I manage my health pretty well I was wondering do you all know anything about Sickle

Cell, would accommodations be made available for me and my disability if I did choose to attend Faulkner?

**Dean Rivera:** Oh yes, Faulkner has many accommodations that can be made for students with disabilities. I am not exactly sure what Sickle Cell is, but I will definitely put you into contact with our front office when the time is right. We have a hospital less than a mile away from the school and a school nurse on hand at all times.

**Nicholas Brooks**: Okay great. That is good to hear, thank you.

**Dean Rivera:** Anything else?

**Nicholas Brooks**: Yeah, I think my biggest concern is my Law School Admission Test score. I think it is pretty low. I have taken it twice already if I take it again and make a higher score will it improve my chances of getting accepted?

**Dean Rivera**: Well Nicholas the LSAT is only one of the few factors we look at when we decide to accept a student. While the better the score the more likely acceptance is, if you think you can do better on the third go around then by all means take it again. But what I want you to know is that it is not the only thing we are looking at, we look at your undergraduate grade point average, your letters of recommendation, volunteering opportunities and even your phone interview plays a role in our final decision.

**Nicholas Brooks:** Okay, well that is good to know. I was really worried about my LSAT score and was not sure if it was enough to get in to a good school.

**Dean Rivera:** That is understandable, Mr. Brooks. I think every student who does not have an LSAT score of 160 or better is concerned about this. Do you have any other concerns?

**Nicholas Brooks:** Yes, how many African Americans are there on campus?

**Dean Rivera**: Well Mr. Brooks I am not sure of a number. The African American students are very active on the law school campus. We actually have a group catered specifically to Black law students. The group is called BLSA which stands for Black Law Students Association.

**Nicholas Brooks**: Oh really? How cool is that? What is there to do in Montgomery entertainment wise?

**Dean Rivera**: Well Faulkner does have a 24-hour gym and a recreation center on campus where intramural sports are played throughout the year. Now I am not sure what there is to do off campus, I have been out of law school for a very long time. But, what I will do is ask some students around your age what they often do and let you know.

**Nicholas Brooks:** Okay great yes, I would like that if it is not too much of a hassle.

**Dean Rivera:** No, not at all that is what I am here for.

**Nicholas Brooks:** Well thank you, I think that is all I have. Thank you for calling me. I hope I did not take up too much of your time.

**Dean Rivera:** No, not at all that is all I have as well. Mr. Brooks if you do not have any more questions then this will conclude our interview. You did great! We will add this to your application folder, review it and you can expect to hear from Jones within 4-6 weeks. We will mail a letter and send an email regarding our decision on your acceptance. Thank you.

**Nicholas Brooks:** Okay look forward to hearing from you. Goodbye!

**Dean Rivera:** Goodbye.

To: Dean Rivera

From: Ralston Jarrett

Date: 3/10/2017

Re: Legally Black Memorandum

**Introduction**

I have been instructed to prepare a legal memorandum to help advise future students on whether Jones School of law located at Faulkner University in Montgomery, Alabama will be the right law school for them. I have been asked to provide insight on the school from my firsthand experience including any relevant information I feel is necessary to make the memorandum informative, clear and concise while addressing the following:

I. What was my motivation for coming to law school?

II. What does it take to be a successful law student?

III. Any other relevant information to help with their law school journey.

People often come to law school for the wrong reasons, and end up dropping out. In this memorandum, I will go into great detail to help not only Jordan and Nicholas with law school, but also any student who is thinking about attending by providing my expertise on law school with the knowledge I have acquired over the last three years. So, here is my memorandum and insight on law school the good, the bad, and the ugly will be discussed.

# Chapter 2

## ARE YOU READY?

**Discussion**

The issue here is whether Jordan and Nicholas are ready to attend law school. Well, let us see if they are ready for the challenge. Are they ready for long nights and early mornings filled with work and hardly ever sleeping? Are they ready to be without their families, spouse and even kids sometimes for the next three years? Are they ready to work during summer vacations? Are they ready for the secondary effects that come with the law school including a poor diet, loss of vision, stress, insomnia, and even depression? Are they ready to be in debt for hundreds of thousands of dollars?

Law school is not like college. College is just a part of your life. The minute you sign the letter of intent, law school becomes your entire life. Law school is your wife. Law school is your husband. This is not a 9:00am-5:00pm Monday through Friday job. You are a law student every day, 24 hours a day, 7 days a week. This is a non-stop job for the rest of your life.

I get approached by a lot about people wanting to go to law school. They are fascinated by the thought of being a future lawyer. People then want to know how I did it. How did this skinny, young, Black, dread-head, from Columbus, Georgia get accepted into law school? Sometimes I think people want me to tell them some type of trick or tactic I used to achieve this, but there is not one. I did what every law student does, worked my butt off.

People then ask what made me come to law school? Money, of course. You can ask 100 law students what is the reason they came to law school and they will all respond with various answers that sound good. But simply put, the main reason people come to law school is for money. There are other reasons of course, to help the community out or to get a better job. Law school is very hard. It will probably be the roughest three years of your life. The only reason a person would endure the unbelievable amount of stress that comes along with law school is for money.

The most common myth about law school that I hear from people is that they would make a good lawyer because they like to argue or they can argue about anything. Is that what most people think we do? If you are contemplating on coming to law school because you like to argue, I will save you $100,000 right now. Go apply to be a manager at a local pawn shop because law school is not for you. A good law student knows the best way to win a case is to win it before even stepping foot in a courtroom. Law schools will not tell you certain things I plan to share. Since neither Jordan nor Nicholas know any lawyers before coming to law school, then this will be of great use to them.

In order to help properly advise Jordan and Nicholas, I will start by laying a proper foundation and building on top of that so they will not think I got into law school overnight. I will start from the very beginning of my life, and end at the present day to give them a full glimpse on who exactly I am, where I come from, and everything I have been through both before and during law school.

## Who is Ralston?

My name is Ralston Jarrett, I attend Thomas Goode Jones School of Law located on the campus of Faulkner University in Montgomery, Alabama. I am not what one would call the typical law student. I am a Black male with dreadlocks and did I mention that I have Sickle Cell Disease? The same disability as Nicholas.

On May 13, 2017, I will have been the first person in the history of the school to graduate with dreadlocks, and I think with Sickle Cell Disease, but there is no way to prove this. The good thing for me and Nicholas is that Sickle Cell does not affect intelligence. The bad thing is it affects everything else. My mind, which is normal, is telling my body, which is not normal, it can do things that it cannot. This is a gift, and a curse, depending on how you look at it. I will get into more detail about managing the painful disease throughout the memorandum, specifically for Nicholas Brooks. As my journey to get to law school and to stay here will be geared toward Nicholas and Jordan.

# Chapter 3

## LAW SCHOOL DREAMS

My law school dreams started at my undergraduate college, Columbus State University. Everyone usually has a professor in college who changes their life. The professor who inspired me to start my legal career was Mrs. King. Mrs. King was a prosecutor from Florida who was teaching Criminal Justice courses as she studied for the Georgia Bar Exam. Mrs. King had a natural liking toward me for some reason, and the feeling was mutual. I had never known a lawyer before I met her, and she would always tell us cool stories about law school and about her being a prosecutor in Florida before moving to Fort Benning, Georgia. Shortly after I met Mrs. King, a friend of mine who I knew from school named Latoya had gotten accepted into Faulkner University's Jones School of Law. These two events were the first time the thought of law school even entered my mind.

A year went by and the thought of law school had come and left my mind, until the winter of 2012 right after the NBA all-star game. I was watching the news and a seventeen-year-old boy had just been shot to death. The shooter, a Hispanic male who was the head of his neighborhood-watch gunned the young man, Trayvon Martin, down for no apparent reason. As I am watching this, a sense of anger takes over my body. The pain on the faces of the young boy's parents was the fuel to my fire. The picture of Trayvon Martin, merely a child, that the news released touched me. I did not know what but I wanted to do something, I wanted to make a difference in the world. At the time, I did not realize how this event that happened in Florida, hundreds of miles from me, would play such a significant role in my life. This was the turning point in my life and a crucial event that inspired me to pursue law school.

# Chapter 4

## WHAT IS SICKLE CELL?

If you are not a doctor explaining Sickle Cell Disease to someone who does not know what it is can be hard. Sickle Cell is a genetic blood disorder that deprives oxygen from vital parts of the body, which can in turn cause pain known as a Sickle Cell Crisis. Furthermore, this disease causes the body to make deformed red blood cells. Instead of red blood cells looking like a circle, as they should, they are shaped like a half moon. I like to think of them as the breakfast cereals Cheerios and Frosted Flakes. Most people have red blood cells which are circular (Cheerios), making it easy for them to flow through their body, while mine are sickled (Frosted Flakes). Because of their irregular shape, they often get stuck in certain parts of my body, restricting the oxygen flow and causing excruciating pain. This is what occurs during a Sickle Cell Crisis. Since blood flows through every part of the body, they can happen anywhere, which sucks. I've experienced crises all the way from the top of my body, around my brain, all the way down to my ankles. The disease is known to shorten one's life span, with the life of a person with the disease being only about 40 to 60 years of age.

While they have medications, there is no worldwide cure as of yet. When I have a crisis, they can usually be treated at home with lots of fluids, pain medication and rest. Although sometimes the episodes will require hospitalization. During hospital stays (which can last from a day to a week) I receive stronger pain medications and usually blood transfusions. Blood transfusions, while not a cure, help me out tremendously. They allow my body to receive regular red blood cells in my body instead of sickled shaped ones. This makes me feel better for a few weeks until my blood runs its course again with the sickled cells it produces and the pain starts again. While they are mostly helpful, transfusions can also be dangerous; you never know how your body will react to receiving someone else's blood.

Although the blood is screened, it can still contain diseases and you also risk the problem of having an iron overload if you receive them too often. The disease is caused from a genetic disorder that is a DNA trait one's parents has passed down to them. For example, my mother has the Sickle Cell Trait and so does my father. While the Sickle Cell Trait is a gene one possesses, people with Sickle Cell Trait usually do not display the severe symptoms as someone with Sickle Cell Disease. Two traits from both parents will give each of their children a 100 percent chance of them having the trait and about a 50 percent chance of the child having the disease. Hence, the reason my sister has the trait and I have the disease. It is not like AIDS or other diseases where it can be passed along to others. The only way I could pass it on would be to my kids. Since I have the disease, I have a 100 percent chance of giving my children at least the trait even if my spouse has neither the trait nor the disease. But, if I procreate with a woman with the trait my kids will most likely have the disease.

For example, Reebe meets Ralston. Reebe has the Sickle Cell Trait, Ralston has the Sickle Cell trait. The first child they have has the Sickle Cell Trait. The second child they have has the Sickle Cell Disease. If any more children were to be procreated by the two, they have about a 50 percent change of another child having the disease. It would be as if they were flipping a coin with heads labeled as "disease" and tails labeled as "trait". They had my older sister, Roxanne, who has the Sickle Cell Trait, and five years later I arrived. I was diagnosed with Sickle Cell Disease at birth.

Because I have Sickle Cell, I like to take life easy, just one day at a time. As a Sickle Cell Survivor or Warrior, as I like to refer to myself, during a Sickle Cell Crisis, I am sometimes hospitalized when the pain is not manageable at my home. I remember one time I was in the hospital because I had just had a Sickle Cell Crisis followed by pneumonia and I was under the influence of narcotics from all the pain medicine I had received. So, this one time I recall myself waking up in the middle of the night in a cold hospital room with a hospital gown on and it was not a soul in sight, except for my mother (who never leaves my side during a hospitalization). I looked over and she had a very sad look on her face.

With me probably just being administered some blood from the local Red Cross to help my body get back to normal and on pain medication, I look over at her and say, "Mom, do you have anything to eat?"

Pain medication often gives me the hunger munchies and I wake up feeling great and not in pain, but I tend to eat everything in sight. Since it was so late the hospital cafeteria was closed, but of course my mom got me some food, like she always does. While eating, I looked at her and noticed something was bothering her. I asked her what was wrong. She looks at me and proceeds to say, "You were definitely supposed to be here."

I look up with a mouth full of food and say, "What makes you say that?" She proceeds to tell me about a time in the early 1980's that she was back home in Detroit, Michigan and she was walking downtown when an old gypsy woman asked for money to read her fortune. The woman told her she would have a son who she would love dearly. A few years go by and she joins the military. Originally, she was set to go to basic training in Florida, but at the last minute her orders had been switched and she was sent to California where my dad was. First, they had my sister. After they discovered she had the Sickle Cell Trait they decided not to have any more kids. Hence the reason my sister and I are 5 years apart. Until this day, my mother swears she was on birth control when I was conceived. Nine months later, on August 15, 1989 I was born. The doctors came in the room and told my parents that I have Sickle Cell Disease, the very thing they were trying to avoid. My mother said she was holding me in her arms and she was sad at first, but then looked down and just smiled at me. The old gypsy woman was right.

I am trying to think of the best way I can describe the pain felt during a Sickle Cell Crisis for someone who does not know about the disease. It is kind of difficult because there is no similar feeling to even compare it to. Have you ever had a paper cut? Okay, yeah it is nothing like that. The only thing I can think of that would even remotely describe the pain I feel is maybe a bee sting. But multiple bee stings, not just one, or maybe a knife wound after someone has been stabbed. It is a deep, throbbing, constant pain. To give an idea of the type of pain this disease causes, the pain medicine Percocet is what is prescribed to patients upon leaving the hospital after recovering from gunshot wounds. Percocet was my best friend, I kept doses of it on hand knowing I could get a Sickle Cell Crisis at any time. It is hard because people always ask what it feels like and I am not sure if anything on earth can be compared to the pain I feel when I am having a Sickle Cell Crisis.

I remember my very first crisis. I was in second grade so I had to be about seven. I told my mom I was not feeling well and because I had cried wolf a few times to stay home from school she did not believe me this particular time. While my memory is vague I remember my dad believing me for some odd reason. Thank God he did. My dad was in the military, so he was usually always gone off somewhere, but this particular time he stayed home with me as I went back to sleep. I woke up in deep pain; My body hurt all over and I could do nothing but cry. My dad picked me up and put me in the front seat of his car. I still remember the car ride to the hospital like it was yesterday because I had never been in that much pain before.. My mom felt terrible. The time she did not believe me is the time I really was in need of her help. We both learned a valuable lesson that day: I learned to never fake a crisis and she learned how serious this disease was that her son will have to deal with for the rest of his life.

The truth of the matter is that these pain crises that I have are inevitable. You know how most people go to the dentist twice a year? That is how I look at going to the hospital. During law school, my Sickle Cell Crisis became as routine as going to the dentist for most people. Once every six months I would wake up in the middle of the night in excoriating pain, barely able to walk. I'd call 911, go to the hospital for a few days, receive blood, hydrate back up, and they'd send me on my way like it was no big deal. Law school was so strenuous; I did not have time to be sick or feel sorry for myself. People have genuine love for me because I always have a positive outlook on life and they say I have a great vibe that I pass off to other people. What can I say? When you have a life-threatening disease, you enjoy life more. You give off good vibes because you appreciate being on this earth more than a person who has not been diagnosed with a life-threatening disease. When I have a Sickle Cell Crisis I usually am in the hospital about five to seven days. That is a lot of time to really think about things and it makes me more grateful. Sickle Cell is a blessing and a curse. One may wonder how Sickle Cell could be a blessing. Without me having Sickle Cell, I do not think I would have come to law school.

When I am in the hospital the fear of not knowing if I am ever going to ever make it out this time is very scary. I constantly try to keep smiling when my family and friends stop by my hospital room to see me. But knowing in the back of your head that this disease is known to shorten your life expectancy and can cause organ failure is a scary thing. Many times, I have to smile to keep from crying. After I am released from the hospital, it is like I am a brand-new man. After these stressful and traumatic instances, I really do stop and smell the roses more often. When you have a greater chance of your time coming sooner rather than later, you seem to enjoy life a little more. Things that I used to get sad or mad about did not seem to matter as much anymore. I started living for myself rather than the material things some people often glamorize. That money I was making at my job while I was stressing did not mean much while I was in the hospital, that girl that rejected me the other day did not seem as important, my car which I worked so hard trying to get did not matter as much as it once did. The only thing that starts to matter are is whether or not I am going to ever be able to get out this hospital.

I hope I did not get too technical, but this was just a brief insight of the complications the disease comes with that I have firsthand knowledge of. I wanted to help advise Nicholas and to give some background on the disease he and I have been diagnosed with.

# Chapter 5

## UPCOMINGS AND SHORTCOMINGS

My parents met in the United States Army. According to my dad, he was a smooth talker and swept my mother off of her feet instantaneously. The way my mom explains it is that she was the new girl on the army base and my father approached her several times asking to take her out. Eventually she said yes, and the two were married within six months of meeting each other.

I always knew I was different as a kid. My parents tried to explain to me the severity of the disease, but it was hard to truly understand at a young age. In my youth, I was good in sports, but I was never fast enough to keep up with the other kids. I would be tired after little to no physical activity. Although they would never let me play football (being that a serious hit to a person with Sickle Cell could be fatal) they always signed me up for recreational basketball. I was always pretty good in basketball, looking back at it I was great considering my condition. But as a kid I did not know the seriousness of this condition, I just wanted to play on the recreational teams with my friends. I remember always being out of breath though after sprinting up and down the court. As every kid athlete, I wanted to play basketball professionally. My basketball dreams died after I did not make my high school team. I think I was trying to be like my father who had played basketball at the collegiate level for a season until joining the army. I think organized sports can be good, but I did feel like as a Black man, a ball was automatically forced into my hand. Contrary to popular belief every black man cannot play basketball. I was actually good though, but sometimes I think the media and society emphasizes that black men have to play sports to be considered someone important.

As I said earlier, Sickle Cell does not affect one's intelligence. It is more of a physical disorder. My body often hurts when I get too hot, too cold, or become dehydrated. Therefore, I always stay with water. If I do not have a bottle of water around me I will lose my mind. Sickle Cell is also the reason I do not smoke or consume alcohol. Smoking deprives the body of oxygen, while alcohol dehydrates. Both are definite disasters for people who have Sickle Cell Anemia.

Nevertheless, I try not to let it dictate too much of my life. Even when I was younger, I always had a brilliant mind and a very vivid imagination. As a child, I was probably one of the best story tellers of my age. I could do this because my brain just works that way, I often day dream and create little movies and short stories in my head.

Besides the very few times I was sick, I had a very normal childhood. After my first crises at the age of seven, the pain crises went dormant until I got to high school. Around the age of 16 the Sickle Cell Crises became more consistent, occurring every few months. My parents let me do everything the other kids did and never let my illness effect my life. That is probably one of the main reasons why I still think I can do stuff my body does not allow.

As I got older I developed my gift of gab, being a military brat I was constantly moving around the country and had to make new friends at every location. I was always funny as far as telling jokes and stories as a kid. We moved around so much I always felt like I had to entertain people and make them like me so I could make new friends. Therefore, I always had a lot of friends wherever I went. I never would have thought that this would follow me into adulthood. From high school, to college, and even now in law school I always have lots of friends because of my versatility and ability to converse with people from all different cultures and backgrounds.

Middle school is when my dad retired from the army and we finally were able to live in one place more than five years. As I mentioned before, high school is where my hoop dreams ended. I had a major Sickle Cell Crisis during basketball tryouts and regurgitated all over the weight room. After that, I got into cars. Since I could not be the hoop star of the school, I decided to be the guy with the really nice car. This was in the early 2000's when the street racing movies were very popular. I had the nicest car in the parking lot: a 1995 Toyota Camry. It had an all decked out body kit, lime green paint with 12-inch subwoofer speakers and chrome wheels. That is what I was known for in high school, having a really cool car. Academically, I was average. I could have done more, but I did enough to get by.

Reflecting on it now, I would always be tired and dehydrated at school, so I would just be ready to go home. The school did not know about my illness, and I did not know that accommodations probably could have been made for me. I was really smart, but after 8 hours of sitting down and not being able to eat and properly hydrate, like I should have been, I would be beat. I would come home and sleep the majority of the time. Junior and Senior years were the worst, I did not like going to school at all. I would get constant Sickle Cell Crises because I was going through my growth spurts around this time. Every time I would have a major crisis it seems like I would come out the hospital a little taller. Eventually, I realized my problem with high school was not the work but the actual school conditions and the inevitable growing pains I went through.

This was further proven when I took the American College Test (ACT) and the Scholastic Aptitude Test (SAT) my scores were above average, which is great since I did not study for them at all. School was not all bad though, I met some of my closet friends in high school. A few of the same ones who would eventually ride with me back to the attempted robbery scene a few years down the line. There was Dontavian, Chris, Robert, Johnny, Brandon, Marcus and many more. I could make another book listing the number of crazy things we would do for fun. Racing was big for us since it was such an adrenaline rush, then we would go to McDonald's and order a Whopper and other crazy things not on the menu just to give the guy at the window a hard time.

One time, we set some newspapers on fire in front of some girl's house one of us liked and rang the doorbell expecting her to come outside in a panic. Her mom came outside instead in a night gown, stomping the fire out and yelling at us while we drove away. We were just kids having fun trying to find our way in the world.

As you know high school does not last forever, and once that was over we all went our separate ways. I convinced Marcus to go off to the army. He was always a hot head who developed a love for guns around the same time I did, so the army seemed like the perfect solution to keep him out of trouble. I wanted to go with him, but the Army would not let me in with Sickle Cell. So, that was out of the picture. You know how most kids want to follow in the same footsteps as their parents? I was not able to do this because of my Sickle Cell therefore, I had to start my own path so I went off to college. I applied for a Historically Black College/University, Albany State, but I did not get accepted. Columbus State, the local university, however did accept me and the rest is history.

## Off to College

College was a great experience for me. I loved it. It was so much better than high school. College was a new world. I was amazed at the whole concept.

You mean to tell me I can pick my own schedule? I can eat at the cafeteria whenever I choose and teachers are not down my back 24/7 telling me to pull my pants up and get to class? The women were beautiful, the campus was nice and no one cared if you do not come to class or not. High school felt like work, college felt like a lifestyle. In high school, you have to be there all day and go home and do more work. In college, you get to go to class at 10:00am and you may not have to come back until 3:00pm or later, and some classes only met two times a week. I loved the freedom college offered compared to the prison mentality high school had instilled in me by forcing my attendance.

Earlier I said if it had not been for Sickle Cell I would not have come to law school. Sickle Cell made me take life more seriously with me discovering I am not immortal due to my constant hospitalizations. I took a straighter path than some of my peers from high school. After we graduated, I realized I could not do "fun things" (fighting, drinking beer and smoking cigarettes) so I simply abstained from those activities. Drinking alcohol, smoking, and even sex sometimes when not hydrated will cause a major Sickle Cell Crisis.

Since my health would not allow me to do any of these things, I would often stay on campus and just go to the library to read, eventually meeting a new circle of friends.

# Chapter 6

## FINDING MYSELF

A friend of mine once described me to a friend of his like this: "Ralston is not really a thug, but he's not lame either. His looks will fool you, but when he starts speaking; you see its something special about him. He's hard to explain with words, but he's cool." I loved this generalized description of me, ever since he told me about the encounter I often tell myself that I cannot be easily described with words.

Growing up I never knew exactly where I fit in, I was too smart for the cool kids, and too cool for the smart kids. When people see me they often think I am a thug. But what is a thug per se? Thugs usually have a lengthy criminal record, right? I have never been arrested. The thing about young Black males is that many of us are not thugs. But unfortunately when we keep hearing that we are thugs by the media and constantly treated like thugs by society, it becomes easy to start thinking this way. I had to come to the realization that I was not a thug, I was a street kid. The difference between the two is that a thug usually has a criminal record, a street kid however, is one who obtains street smarts from the urban community from which he is from. Many people, especially at predominately white higher institutions of learning were not used to this. I was not a gang banger, I was not an Uncle Tom nor was I the "Carlton Banks" preppy, nerd type- I was just being myself. I never quite understood the logic of conforming to something you are not in order to be accepted by a certain group of people. Do I have long dread locks? Yes. Do I like wearing Jordan's? Yes. Do I like loud rap music? Yes. Do I like nice cars with nice wheels on them? Yes. Do I like to attend strip clubs from time to time? Yes. Does any of that make me a thug or bad person? No, of course not. But after a while you get used to it. I eventually stopped asking why people would look at and treat me differently, like it was illegal to be black or something, and just accepted it for what it was, embracing those who liked me and steering clear of the ones who did not.

## Young and Black

Around the time I was preparing for law school this guy I grew up with was on the news for a high-speed chase. He and some acquaintances (I will not call them friends because friends do not encourage each other to break the law) broke into someone's house, got caught, and lead the police on a high-speed chase. That hit me hard. I grew up with this guy; he was one of my friends, he was younger than I, but I knew he was a good guy who came from a nice family. I ran into him a few years later and asked him what happened. He said it was hanging out with the wrong crowd and making bad decisions. He said he wished he would have just joined the military or enrolled in school like I had. Hanging out with the wrong crowd turned him into a criminal and now he is a convicted felon for the rest of his life.

It is hard living in America when you are young and Black. As a youth, the only people I had to look up to were rappers and basketball players. I was eventually brainwashed into thinking this was the only way for me to be successful. I even tried to be a rapper at one point of time. Back in college, people would often tell me I looked like Lil Wayne, so this went to my head. I got a microphone, a notepad, a chain -all the essentials a rapper needed. There was only one problem, I could not rap. My rap career ended the one night at the college party when I thought I had gotten shot. After that, I stopped partying as much and started to hit the books harder.

This section is specifically for Nicholas, not only as a future law student, but from one Black male to another. Everyone will have a turning point in their life when they will decide what is next for them. I believe his turning point occurred when his brother went to jail. I do not personally know him yet, but I am proud of him for applying to law school. I know the number of hurdles and adversity Black men face every day. My advice to him would be to stay on a straight path, trouble is so easy to get into but very hard to get out of. The story of his brother reminded me of my friend who made the bad decision to hang with the wrong crowd, along with so many other young Black males I know. From his interview, I get a sense that Nicholas is unsure of how he will fit in with the other law students. I would tell him not to fit in at all. The great thing about Jones School of Law is the different backgrounds and cultures of all the students in one school. While we are all different in numerous ways, the things we all have in common is respect for one another and a respect for the law.

# Chapter 7

## MEASURING UP

Growing up I always wanted to be like my big sister, Roxanne, who is five years older than me. My sister is way smarter than I am and I consider myself a smart guy. I always tease her for me having to get braces. When we were kids we were outside playing and due to her lack of paying attention, one of her childhood friends ran me over with a bike knocking out all of the baby teeth I had and causing my adult teeth to grow back in crooked.

But one thing about my sister is she would always have my back and would go against anyone for me. No one could mess with me and get away with it while Roxanne was around. I recall one time in middle school this one kid was bothering me, and somehow my sister found out. She walked over from the high school and cursed the poor boy out. To have such an age difference, we were always very close. Due to the fact that my parents were working all the time, and us moving so much, we were best friends because we were all each other had. Due to our age difference, we only went to school together twice in our lives. Once was in elementary school; I was in first grade and she was in fifth, and the other would be in college at Columbus State.

I see that Jordan's brother is a doctor, those are big shoes to fill. I am sure many younger siblings would agree that it is hard being a younger sibling. As a younger sibling, you are always expected to measure up to the older sibling and you never get a finder's fee. When I say a finder's fee, I mean that everything done as a second child is good, but of course not as great as it is with the first child. And as a younger sibling, you always suffer the consequences of the mistakes the first child has done. I do not even think my parents realized that and probably did not even mean to do this. It is like going to the movies. If you see the movie one time it is a great experience, now when you watch that movie again it is still good, but it is just not as exciting as the first go around. For example, my kindergarten graduation was great, but they had already been to my sisters. My fifth-grade graduation was a good event, but my sister had already done it. My first day of high school, while still exciting, had also already been done. The purchasing of a car, even my high school graduation and college graduation were both the same. Family is still happy for you, but it's just not the same thrill the second time it is done.

Not only was I living in my sister's shadow in my school life, but in my social life as well. My sister is really pretty and smart, so she was always popular. Me on the other hand, I was not very known or if they knew me it was as, "Roxanne's brother". My sister was such a good student that when I would go to a new school I would already be expected by the teachers who had taught her to be an excellent scholar as well. This was a lot of pressure. It went on from elementary school until college where some of the professors would see my last name and ask, "Jarrett? Are you related to Roxanne Jarrett?"

Law school was the only thing that my sister had not done. I was stepping out of my big sister's shadow. This opportunity would not only provide a better life for my family and I, it also allowed me to identify who I was and what I was good at without the feeling of having to measure up to my smarter older sister. Law school finally gave me my own name that was not just "Roxanne's little brother" anymore.

My advice to Jordan is to make sure her heart is in her decision to come to law school. In her phone interview, I get a sense that she and her brother are very close because they have been through so much together. But my concern is whether Jordan is doing this journey for herself or trying to compete with or even fill the shoes of her older brother who is a doctor. Measuring up to an older sibling, a parent, or anyone is hard. It is a common source of failure in law school. Many people attend law school because a relative has made them attend, a parent is a lawyer, or a sibling is a lawyer or another type of professional. This is often a recipe for disaster; When one's heart is not truly into law school and they come for the wrong reasons; they usually do not make it past the first semester. If her decision to attend is made from the heart because she wants to help children get adopted, then this should be the motivation she uses to get in and stay in law school, and she will have made a good decision in coming to Jones School of Law

# Chapter 8

## DREADLOCS

Many people do not know that I am Jamaican. My dad was born in Kingston in the 1950's and eventually came to the United States. I have been growing my "locs" (as I will refer to them herein) out since 2006. The irony behind this is that my dad was very against me dreading my hair. He is retired military and he has always had a low cut. I have always had a strong mind and very hard head, as some may say. He told me not to get them, and I went and got them anyway. My mom was more open minded to things like this, although she never understood why I wanted locs since my hair is very soft and curly and not really the ideal texture for locs. Around the time I started growing my locs, I was about sixteen years old, trying to find myself and learn more about my heritage. To top it off, my favorite rappers had locs, Lil Wayne and Pastor Troy, so I emulated those guys because I thought they were cool. I am also a huge Bob Marley fan, so there were several things which played a part in my decision. Against my father's wishes, I kept the locs. My father, as with many other members of the older generation, did not understand this new generation. As people get older they can sometimes forget the things they did when they were younger. History seems to repeat itself, just in different and modern ways. In the 70's it was afros, in the 80's it was jheri curls, in the 90's it was high top fades and in the 2000's it was dreadlocks. The ironic part is that my father would constantly tell me stories about his parents getting onto him about something but could never see that he was doing the same exact thing. Looking back, I see my father was just trying to protect me from the many stereotypes that come with having locs. As bad as he wanted, he could not protect me from the dangers of the world. Even if I had a low haircut, I still would be young, Black and considered a threat to anyone who was not accustomed to Black men, that was something my father could not protect me from.

After having locs for over 10 years, I have heard hurtful things from not only other races but from fellow African Americans as well. White people were more curious and infatuated with them, and would often ask to touch them, which I absolutely hated. It was the other African Americans who have given me the most grief and actually have the audacity to say certain things to my face. I do understand many people, especially other races, may think the same thing, but they usually are not brave enough to say it directly to my face. I have heard numerous times from African American women that they do not talk to "dread heads" because they are trouble. I have also been asked numerous times how I was going to be a lawyer with dreads and before that, how I was going to be in law school with dreads. I think prejudices from your own race hurts twice because they come from people who look like you and should understand the struggle of being Black. Fortunately for me, I am very stubborn and hard headed. I knew I was not the type to conform in order to fit in. Quite frankly, if Faulkner would not have let me in because of a hairstyle, I would have applied somewhere else.

People would often tell me, "It's just hair, cut it." Maybe to them it was hair but to me it was more. My locs were a part of who I was, they were a part of my Jamaican heritage, and I refused to let anyone change who I was in order to conform to their standards. A lady once told me, "I don't know if I would hire a lawyer with dreads?" I politely responded by asking why? After she gave some excuse with no rationale on how one's hair could possibly affect the outcome of her case, I told her not to hire me then. If you want to hire a lawyer for his looks then you are doomed from the start, and not a person who I would want to work with anyhow. But she, along with many other people, have this stigma that all Black lawyers must look like the late Johnny Cochran. I am not Johnny Cochran, I do not want to be Johnny Cochran. My hope is to eventually break that stigma. Who says you must look a certain way to be a good lawyer?

## Stay true to yourself

My stubbornness about cutting my hair came from when I read the Autobiography of Malcolm X. In it he describes how he would perm his hair to make it straight like the hair of white people. He did this for many years until he suddenly realized that by doing this, he and everyone else who try to change their hair to conform to European standards were essentially saying that the white race was "superior" and that Black people were "inferior" because we are altering our hair ultimately to conform to standards in hopes of being accepted. I loved it, and ever since then, I refused to let anyone tell me how I must look or wear my hair.

The first and only time I had to confront someone in law school about my locs happened during summer classes after my first year. One of my professors made a rude comment pertaining to my hair. In my first year of law school I would often have my locs tied to the back, or have them in a man bun. Since it was summer, I came to school with my locs hanging down and a fitted hat. On this particular day, I got to class early and everyone was there waiting on the professor. He walked in and he looked at me and says something to the effect that my hair being down scared him. I was furious, would he have said that to a white man with long hair? Probably not. The other students were all looking like *can you believe he said that* and one of my friends (who was bald) tried to make light of the situation and made a joke like "I wish I could grow hair like Ralston's." I just laughed it off and act like it did not bother me. I approached him after class, telling him how I did not appreciate his comment and I found it to be offensive. He apologized and that was that. I think Faulkner had to adjust to me, just as I had to them.

My advice to Nicholas and Jordan is just be true to yourself. If people do not like you because of the way you look, then it is their loss and they missed out on probably getting to know a great person. If one judges people off of race, gender, attractiveness, or even a hairstyle then that person is shallow and probably is not a good friend anyway. I also want to emphasize that you cannot always listen to what other people say. If I had listened to everyone, then I would not be the first dread head to graduate from Jones School of Law. What if I had cut my dreads off because I felt like it was not professional looking or I had listened to people who had told me I could not be a lawyer with dreads? Sometimes you have to do your own thing, you have to walk through the crowd with headphones on. When I say that I mean many people in your life, family, friends, and acquaintances, will always give their opinion on your life. But remember, not all advice is good advice. Block out all the different people offering their two cents and walk through the crowd with your headphones on, meaning continue to do what you want in life and whatever feels right to you.

# Chapter 9

## STAYING OUT OF TROUBLE

The night I knew I had to leave my hometown of Columbus was the first time I had ever pulled my weapon out on someone. I had just graduated from college and went to a college party where I met a young woman. We talked back and forth and I finally went to go see her. She stayed in a rough part of town, and going against my better judgement, I went over there at night. It was a dark night in some Columbus housing projects, I had my pistol on me, (as I always did ever since the night of the attempted robbery). So, I went over pistol on my waist and we are talking, laughing, and then a knock on the door happens. I did not pay any mind to it at first seeing as this was my first time visiting her. My demeanor changed as I saw the look on her face change when she looked to see who was out there. When she saw who it was at the door the expression on her face turned to horror.

She then proceeded to tell me that she was in an abusive relationship. I am thinking *oh now you tell me*, and while she was done with him, he obviously was not done with her by the way he was violently banging on the front door. So, I was calmly sitting on the couch watching television waiting on him to leave so I can exit. There must have been a hole in the blinds or something because somehow, he saw me sitting on the couch. My plan was going well until I heard him on the phone talking to one of his friends.

"Aye Pooch, go on the back porch and bring me the bag with the K in it." (A "K" is street slang for an AK-47 assault rifle). That was all I needed to hear. I popped up immediately, pulled my pistol from my waistband and cocked it. I opened the door and the guy looked at me, swearing and acting rambunctiously, until he saw the cocked pistol in my hand and you can suddenly see all the confidence and anger leave out of his body as he retreated.

I tried to step outside to leave, not chase him. The girl who I had come to see and her sister would not let me go out. I do not know what I would have done if he had come at me, but I knew that I was not going to sit around lying in wait for his friend to bring him the bag he was so frantically talking about. A few minutes passed, and I left. I proceeded with caution to my car, gun drawn.  I drove off and kept that story pretty much a secret until now.

The lesson I learned that night was to be prepared because your life can change at any moment. I used to watch all of the crimes stories and hear about local news story and think that people were dumb. After that night, I was always a little more empathic. I could see how someone could say just a few words and it could have you ready to make a bad decision in a split second. The thing with life though is, once the decision is made, it is not like a video game where you can rewind it and start over. Imagine if that girl did let me go outside that night and he tried to fight me and I had to shoot him. I could easily be in prison and not law school. Or, imagine if his friend was just around the corner and was able to get to him in a hurry; Where would I be now?

After that night, I vowed to never try to put myself in that kind of predicament again. I was not going back to the projects any more. I did not care how fine the girl was, and more importantly, I learned to follow my first mind. I knew better to go on that side of town at night by myself, but I still did. I never told my parents about this incident. My mom would've just been super worried, and my dad, although he was a man, would not have understood how it is with the new generation. My dad grew up in the 1970's. Back then, you could survive without a gun; everybody would fist fight or have a dance or singing battle if there was ever a dispute. But in this generation, it is very different. It is a shoot first or get shot mentality. Guys will bust your head, beat you and rob you just because they feel like it. For me, carrying a gun meant having power, but as we all know, too much power in the wrong hands is never a good thing. Fortunately, I have never had to shoot anyone. Have I had to draw my weapon? Yes. But it was always in self-defense, never as an aggressor. I know it is probably hard to imagine me being even remotely violent, but it has happened from time to time. I am here to tell you it is hard to reason with a man while a gun is pointed at you. It is sad that the streets instilled this "hurt-or-be hurt" attitude within me. Between the attempted robbery, someone trying to car jack me previously, and being in the midst of a possible shootout because some guy is angry at his ex-girlfriend, I knew I had to do something before I got into some serious trouble. After those few incidents, I knew I had to leave Columbus, and it was around this time that. I cut out all the distractions and I started studying for my first attempt at the LSAT. (Law School Administration Test).

These encounters are specifically for Nicholas, while my hometown, Columbus, Georgia, is probably not as rough as the south side of Chicago, I do know how life in the inner city can be. It is hard. My advice for him would be to stay out of trouble because it is hard to get out of, and keep the distractions to a minimum. Women, friends, and sometimes even family can be a distraction when you are trying to achieve a goal such as this. If he is accepted to Jones School of Law, the move to Montgomery to attend Faulkner would be great for him. The city of Montgomery will slow him down and minimize his distractions and the possibility of getting into any trouble. Unlike my father, I completely understand how this generation is. It is very easy to get into trouble, even when you are not necessarily looking for it.

Unfortunately, people who know you are a good person just trying to do the right thing will really try to bring you out of your character. Although I do not have a brother, I can empathize on how he felt when his brother went to jail for a crime he did not commit. But I want him to see that his life can instantly change just as fast. All his hard work can be washed away from one rash decision. I hope he took the lesson from his brother's past experience to heart and sees that if he wants to make a change, not only for himself but for his community, he should stay focused, maintain his health and avoid distractions in order to take the opportunity to come to Jones School of Law.

# Chapter 10

## PREPPING FOR LAW SCHOOL

College was the first time I found my love for the law. I was originally a theatre major, then I changed it to physical education, and finally to criminal justice. I took the Introduction to Criminal Justice course as an elective and did fairly well. So, I decided to stick with it because it was easy for me and I was naturally intrigued about law. It felt good to know my rights and the procedure to follow if I were to ever get arrested.

During my last semester of college, I did my internship at the Columbus Felony Probation Office. I definitely suggest interning or job shadowing before you decide if you want to do something as a full-time career. I worked at the probation office for several months. It was not exactly what I thought it to be. While some of the officers were there to help rehabilitate, some of the other probation officers were bullies. As the internship ended they offered me a job at the office, but there was a catch: I would have to cut my dreadlocks off. The job started off at $33,000, health insurance, 401k, and everything else I could imagine.

On my last day there, right before I was set to graduate college, one of the probationers keyed my car. The scratches from the keys were really deep, and I had to pay for a professional to repaint the entire side of my car. That incident was it for me. I had been thinking about coming to work for the probation office until that happened. I was so angry at everyone that I decided not to return. Besides the fact of my practically brand new Challenger getting vandalized, deep down in my heart I knew if I would have taken that position I would be selling myself short. Looking back at the incident of the keying of my car was just an excuse I made up to justify why I would turn down a job that paid over thirty thousand dollars a year to chase my dreams of going to law school. But, what can I say? I am a big risk taker and the turning down of this job was definitely one of the biggest risks I have ever taken.

My advice to Jordan and Nicholas would be to have a backup plan. If they have a previous job or career, it is often hard to leave a guaranteed salary for something that is not guaranteed. This is just one of the many risks associated with law school. I knew I wanted to go to law school, but if I would not have gotten accepted, I still had a job at the probation office. The sad truth about law school is that not everyone will get accepted, and even out of those who are accepted, not everyone will make it through the first year. The first day of orientation the staff instructs you to look to your left, then to your right. "One of you three will not make it the entire three years." Therefore, it is always best to have a backup plan in case law school does not work out.

## The Process

Many people do not know this, but my law school acceptance did not happen overnight. The process of applying to law school was very strenuous and required patience. I took the LSAT a total of three times before I received my first acceptance letter. The first time I took the test, I tried to self-teach and did horrible. The second time, I got some help. I took an LSAT prep course that Auburn University offered. I would study from 9:00am to 12:00pm Monday through Friday, then go to work at the Boys and Girls Club. From there, I'd drive to Auburn University three times a week, which is about 45 minutes from Columbus, Georgia. I had to drive there an back, which meant a total of 90 minutes per day just driving. After all of that, I took the test for the second time, and I did not get the score I wanted. So then, I took both the course and the test again.

Studying for law school is very hard. Do not try to teach this material to yourself. You may as well look at a French book and try to teach yourself a foreign language. Unless you are a complete genius and can teach yourself how to master new things, then I highly recommend a LSAT prep course. These preparation courses teach skills and tactics to help you do better. While the courses are expensive, I still consider it one of the best investments I have ever made. The prep course taught me how to think and analyze properly enough to do well on the test and that is all I cared about. I did not care about the cost.

The course I took had a money back guarantee, so I did not have much to lose. The cost was a little over $1000 and they had an online course for a little cheaper. I paid it. What was $1000? I would spend $250 on a pair of Air Jordan's on any given weekend. What was a $1000 to get me ready for the hardest test I had ever taken?

This is what will separate you from the millions of people who want to go to law school and the few thousand who actually do make the cut. You have to be willing to invest in yourself. Take the money for the Jordan's you were going to buy next Saturday and invest it.

Months went by and I received my results: a 145 out of 180, and I was disappointed. I wanted at least a 150. The LSAT does not have a passing score but the higher you score, the more likely you are to be accepted into a law school. With the support of my family, I wiped myself off and headed right back to the library. Much to my surprise, while studying, I received an acceptance letter from Thomas Goode Jones School of Law in Montgomery, Alabama.

## The Balancing Test

In the months preparing to go to law school the jitters started to arrive. I was going to have to leave my job and everything I had known for the past couple of years to embark on a journey that I was not sure I was ready for. What if I was not smart enough? Can I afford this? Many questions like that will come to mind when making a life changing decision such as this one. My decision to attend law school was done with something I call "The Balancing Test" I usually do the test before making any major decision. I would get a piece of paper and write down all the positive things that would come from a situation, and on the other side of the paper; I would write down all the things I could lose from the decision. If the pros outweighed the cons I would do it. If they did not, then I would not. On the left the pros: another degree, better job opportunities, respect in the community, a chance to help people, better financial stability in the future. On the right the cons: possibly flunking out of school, having to step out of comfort zone.

Ultimately, I did decide to go, and it ended up being one of the best decisions I ever made in my life. I say this to say, in all aspects of your life you are going to be faced with some type of decision. Do not be afraid. Think about them rationally, get some advice from the right people, think about it more if you need to, then just do it. After thinking about it and looking at The Balancing Test, I just prayed and signed the letter of intent. My gut feeling was telling me to take the opportunity, and I did. I am the type of person to overthink something and talk myself out of it. With law school, I had to just jump in because no one has ever made history playing it safe. That afternoon, with the letter of intent signed I officially became a law student.

The best advice to give to Jordan and Nicholas is not to be cheap when it comes to law school. Unless you are a genius you will either have to take a prep course or hire a tutor or something, especially if your LSAT score is not where you want it to be. The LSAT is important, but it is not the end of the world if your score is not as high as you wanted it to be. If Nicholas wants to take the LSAT again, the test is offered multiple times a year and he should look into getting an LSAT prep course. I know they're expensive, but I do not think I would have been able to get into law school without it. Don't be discouraged. I took the LSAT three times and was preparing to take it again. Everyone is different; some people will have to take it more than once. When I was preparing to take the LSAT, I felt as if I was fighting three battles at the same time. One against the everyday struggles that come from being young and black, the second with my health and the constant fight with it, and the third with the new stress that the LSAT was bringing. If Jordan wants to be a lawyer, she will have to jump out on a limb and not play it safe in Woodbury. Tell her to use my "Balancing Test" if she must, but it is quite normal to start second guessing yourself and your decision. I would encourage her to talk to her fiancé, her brother, and other family members whose opinion she values. If she is still not sure, then tell her just to go for it, take the risk, nothing great ever comes from playing it safe.

# PART II

# Chapter 11

## LAW SCHOOL

The worst thing I can do is to sugar coat this experience for Jordan and Nicholas. Law school is very hard to say the least. They need to get this visual in their heads: every person in law school is smart. Everyone has done fairly well in their undergraduate college studies to have made it to this level. Law school is really the best of the best competing against one another. Just because they were excellent students at their college does not mean they will be a great student in law school. The competition is fierce. Our graduating class began with 108 people, however we will only graduate with 78 people.

While some people have transferred schools, most people have dropped out. I have even heard rumors about people having to drop out and check in to mental health facilities immediately after. Many people are not cut out for the strenuous environment and do not make it past the first semester. Not knowing anyone who had ever attended law school was a disadvantage for me. Naturally, this will be a disadvantage for Jordan and Nicholas as well. The competition they will be up against are students whose parents and grandparents are lawyers and judges, so they will have already had an introduction into the legal field. As I mentioned earlier, the people from the new incoming class will have been breed for law school and probably knew they were coming their entire life. While Jordan and Nicholas will be strangers to a brand-new world and be thrown to the wolves.

Law school is very competitive. Our grades are given on a curved grading system. The way our school is set up, there can only be one "A" given per class which is the top paper. After that "A" the rest of the papers are scaled from it. The next best papers will be A minuses and the next will be in the B plus range. This continues until someone is given an F. This is the worst paper in the class. Confusing, right? I will elaborate in greater depth. Law school is a competition, therefore the school has to weed out people who they feel will not pass the bar. The higher bar passage rate a school has, the higher the law school will be ranked, and more people will want to attend the law school. So, this is the rationale for the extensive pressure the professors put on us and the reason for the harsh dismissal policies. This is what makes law school such a scary place. The fact that people know that some classmates must be academically dismissed before the year is over puts fear in people.

Law school has its own disciplinary court proceedings called Honor Court. This is where people who have been accused of plagiarism, cheating, acting unethical, and broken other rules in the Faulkner Law Rule Handbook are brought. These proceedings are held like a real trial and can get someone kicked out of school or placed on a probationary period. The students act as lawyers, the jury, and the judge to determine whether someone is guilty or not. Fortunately for me, no one in my section turned people's names into honor court. There were many instances in the other sections where people were telling on others and bringing them up on honor court charges. This kind of thing can ruin a law student's career before it starts due to the fact that when preparing to sit for one's state bar, you are asked have you ever been brought up on honor court charges while in law school: If so, you must explain to the state bar committee why you were accused of the misconduct. It will then be up to the state bar committee to decide if they will allow you practice law in the state.

Something that was a big shock to me was the attendance policy. Law school is a professional stepping stone. To get ahead, one must act like a professional and conduct themselves in a professional manner. While some professors will let someone walk in a few minutes late, other professors will not allow it. If one was late they did not get to sign the attendance roll, if the attendance roll does not get signed you get an absence for the day and four absences result in you failing the class.

The next thing that came as a surprise to me was the responsibility to read the cases for the next class period. In law school, one must brief cases we are assigned to read and then elaborate the facts and significance of the case to not only the professor; but to the entire class. The selection of each name is random, and the consequence of getting kicked out for not being prepared is totally at the discretion of the professor. If one is not prepared, they can get put out of class and counted absent for the day.

## Networking

If one is not willing to endure the difficult process of preparing for the entrance exam, then more than likely they will not be willing to put in the work necessary to be successful in law school and as a lawyer. If I could go back and change one thing before coming to law school, I would have networked more in the legal world in Columbus. While I was in college, I was an after-school tutor for children at a Martial Arts Institution. I did this for several years, and I thoroughly enjoyed it. But, I wish I would have known someone who went to law school and could have told me that a job down in the courthouse would not only be beneficial to my future law school career, but would also allow me to network .Therefore, if I ever did decide to practice in Georgia I would know everyone from the law clerks, to the lawyers, to the judges.

When I applied to law school, it was solely off of hope and a prayer. There's a saying that goes "it is not always what you know, but who you know." This is very accurate, many of my classmates had worked as paralegals, interns, clerks and other jobs in the legal field. Therefore, had an upper hand on me when it came to legal writing and research. I did attend multiple law school fairs when I was applying to different schools across the country. Similar to job fairs, a law school fair is an event where law schools from all over the country come in one building and pass out pamphlets and cards in hopes of you applying to their school. I would google law school fairs and find the dates they were coming and get in the car to go. The nearest ones would be in Auburn, Alabama about 45 minutes away from my hometown of Columbus, Georgia. These law schools receive hundreds to thousands of applications a year, so when they saw my application, they would be able to look out for me.

"Oh, that's Ralston, I met him at the law school fair. He was a nice young man, let me look at his application." One must have extreme dedication as the process of applying to law school will not be easy.

A funny story that shows my dedication occurred during my second year of law school when I started shadowing a juvenile lawyer here in Montgomery. I would go to court maybe two or three times a month. To make a good impression on the attorneys downtown, I would wake up every morning and go get donuts from Dunkin Donuts. Court started at 8:30 am, I lived 30 minutes away from the courthouse and the only Dunkin Donuts in town was ten minutes away from my house. I would be up about 6:45am in order to arrive around 7:50 am so the lawyers could have the donuts before 8:30am when court started. This is an example of the type of dedication one must have in order to be successful in the legal field. It got to a point where they were like Donuts again? But my plan worked, I made great connections, and I was offered an internship there.

My advice to Jordan and Nicholas would be to start networking in your home towns now. If you have to take an internship, do it! Everything will not be paid, starting off you may have to volunteer, but while you may not receive any monetary benefits, I guarantee you the lifelong connections will be beneficial to you in the long run. I notice that a lot of people are so worried about making a dollar that they pass up great opportunities that would benefit them in the long run. Check your local Government Websites. Law clerks are always needed. Call a lawyer and tell him/her you are interested in law school and ask if they need a receptionist, an assistant, anything to get you noticed and your foot inside of the legal door. Do not wait until you get into law school to start meeting local attorneys and judges. If Jordan and Nicholas plan on going back to their hometowns to practice law, then right now is the perfect time to get acquainted with the lawyers of their city. Do not take the summer before you come to law school off to relax. Get out and meet people so when you come back next summer, you will already have an internship waiting on you due to keeping in contact with the people you met the previous summer.

# Chapter 12

## ONE L OF A YEAR

My first year of law school was my worst year. In law school, you are classified by the number of years you have been in the school. Law school is generally three years if you enter into a full-time program. So, my first year I was a 1L ,meaning a first-year law student. As you progress in school you then become a 2L, and 3L.

On my first day of law school I wore a brand-new suit my parents had bought me. I am walking on campus looking lost and Mrs. Golden, (who I call my law school mom) saw me and gave me the biggest hug in the world. This made me feel better. Mrs. Golden works in the Admissions Office, so she knew everything about me from my social media, applications, my telephone interview and my personal statement long before I ever stepped on campus. I will never forget her first words to me, "Ralston! You are even cuter in person. That face belongs on a television screen I tell you!"

Mrs. Golden is one of the few people who never stereotyped me. She stills goes out of her way to speak to me even in a room full of crowded people. While Mrs. Golden was welcoming, some of the students and other faculty members were not so friendly.

During the first couple of weeks of school everyone started to form cliques while I was alone. The looks I received my first semester of law school were horrific. People's body language and facial expressions will tell you more than their mouths will ever say. I knew I was going to have to prove myself; I was aware of that, I had been doing it all my life. People are always afraid of the unfamiliar. I love my classmates now, but we got off to a rocky start. I did not worry about it too much. I had met a few people, I knew the rest of the class would come around eventually. I was used to being around different cultures because of my dad being in the military and attending schools with a variety of people. But, I do not think a lot of people at Faulkner had seen a guy quite like me before. I received some of the worst looks you could ever imagine. The ones who did not look disgusted or frightened by my presence just ignored me. Looking back at it now, I did nothing wrong but be unapologetically black. If being young and black with swagger on a law school campus was a crime, then I was guilty. Young, slim, and a head full of dreadlocks that was me. To make matters worse, not only were the white students looking at me strange, so were the black students. After a while I got used to it, I eventually stopped caring how or why people were looking at me. While I do not want to paint a racist picture of the campus and accuse them all of being bigots, I would definitely be lying if I told you it was fine, race did not matter, and everyone welcomed me with open arms, and we have been a big happy family ever since day one.

## Getting Acquainted

My first day on campus was scary. Contrary to popular belief, I am a shy and quiet guy, especially in a new environment. After my brief encounter with Mrs. Golden, no one spoke to me for the first several hours of orientation. It was not until I was eating lunch by myself when Mike came and introduced himself to me. Mike was cool. He was a white guy, with prior military service from Florida. We talked about our plans on becoming lawyers. While he wanted to be a prosecutor, I told him I wanted to do criminal defense. Mike was alright, he was actually the first student I met at school and we have remained good friends. Sandra was the second person I met. She was an older black lady. I liked Sandra because she reminded me of my mother. She came and introduced herself to me after she had seen me sitting alone. My start on campus was definitely a rocky one with the rest of the students and the faculty. I had a few friends who had introduced themselves to me including Mike, Sandra and Stephen who ended up being one of my best friends during my 1L year, but I was definitely not like the others who were already divided by the different cliques they had formed.

Stephen was an Asian guy who was an ex-marine. He smoked marijuana and was a Bob Marley fan, so we hit it off instantly. I cannot remember exactly how Stephen and I met, but I remember we had a few classes together and eventually just became friends. Stephen was from Texas and would remind you of it any chance he got. He had been over to Iraq in the war and had gotten out of the military to pursue law school.

## Problems back at home

Meanwhile while I was making new friends here, my old friends were calling me with bad news. I got a call one night that one of my best friends Chris had just gotten a gun pulled on him. I guess I was not supposed to be there because Chris and I were always together until I left for Montgomery and the first time he was in trouble; I was gone. After that another friend of mine Kedar had gotten into a fight at a party. I felt bad that there was nothing I could do. On top of all this a friend of mine named Denzel had died. He was playing a pickup basketball game and collapsed. I wanted to come home to attend his funeral but unfortunately, I could not make it. The amount of work I was receiving in law school was astounding. I had never had this amount of work in college. I start regretting my decision on coming, I was not there for my friends in their times of need and I was not able to attend a funeral for a good friend of mine. Not only was it my friends, but then my family started to have problems. My uncle was sick for a while. He was excited to see me go off to law school when I told him I had got accepted. He was sick, but every time I would go visit him his eyes would light up. My visits had gradually decreased naturally as I started my 1L year. He passed soon after. Law school will often make you feel guilty for putting it's needs before those of your own, your family, and friends.

## Crisis time

In the meantime, back in Montgomery I was adjusting to the new environment. The first week of law school was over and its going well until I had a Sickle Cell Crisis. My second week of law school I was in the hospital. Every time a big change in my life happens I have a major Sickle Cell Crisis. I had one during my first week of college as well. So, I missed about three days of classes and returned. While most people did not even acknowledge my absence. One girl came up to me and said "Oh you are back? I thought you had quit." Stephen had called a few times to check up on me while I was in the hospital. He called and texted me every day until I returned and even took all the class notes I had missed and sent them to me. As the weeks ensued I start getting the hang of law school.

## Getting Comfortable

For the first few weeks of my 1L year I was wearing a suit every day. One day I started to realize only I and a few other Black people were the only ones still dressed up. Everyone else were starting to dress casually. I was already not comfortable wearing a suit every day, it was hot and a hassle to iron and lay out a different one each night. So, I started wearing more casual wear. My casual wear was a little different from the casual wear other students were wearing. They all looked the same. They usually had on polo shirts, cargo shorts and boating shoes. You would think this was the unofficial uniform for law students. My comfortable wear including polo shirts, cargo shorts and Jordan's. If we are being frank people were stereotyping me from the first day I stepped on campus. Me wearing a suit did not change their perceptions of me so now, I just dressed how I wanted.

Another factor that played a part in the constant stereotypes was my car. I had a 2010 dodge challenger it was all white, on white twenty-two inch wheels. Since I was quiet and did not speak to many people (except for the few I knew) a rumor on campus began to spread that I was a drug dealer. It is a common misconception that young Black men cannot have worked for nice things and had to have done something illegal to obtain anything nice. I hate this, but I thought my classmates were more mature than that. The challenger was simply a college graduation gift. I suppose it just comes with being young and black I say that because my friend Josh a 1L at the time as well had a very nice Nissan 350z and there were no rumors of him being a drug dealer. We are the same age, come from very similar households the only difference is he is white and I am Black.

My future best friend Tiff, who I did not know at the time told me she even thought I was a drug dealer. I asked her why and she was said she did not know just assumed it was true because everyone was saying it. I was amazed, I kind of expected that from other students, but not from the other Black people. The irony of it all is that the campus drug dealer is a white lady who you would never think did anything illegal in her entire life. Adderall and marijuana were very popular with students during my first year of law school. There was always peer pressure to engage in these activities because they will "make you study better" but I never did.

## Keeping Secrets

Before I came off to law school I had received a handicapped decal from my doctor. I would go to the front of the school and park in the handicap parking area near the entrance of the school while other students would be in the parking lot fighting on limited parking. The handicap decal was great. I used it to alleviate some of the walking I had to do each day on the way to class, especially in the dangerously hot temperatures. If people did not like me already, they really did not like me after they saw I was the first one in class sitting down without a look of exhaustion on my face. I know people will probably wonder why I did not tell them I had Sickle Cell. It was none of their business, I as with many other Sickle Cell patients are very private with our health issues. Upon meeting, someone it is not one of the first things you want to say to someone. I personally do not like the pity that comes after telling someone I have Sickle Cell. If you were a jerk to me before you found out I had it, continue to be one. Then people will usually try to empathize and make it worse. "I had a cousin who died from sickle cell" and the rudest comment I have heard "are you going to die?" People can be ignorant sometimes so I do not like to talk about it too much. As, crazy as this may sound I would have rather been the "thug" or "drug dealer" on campus then to be known as the Sickle Cell Boy.

## Help a brother out?

First semester of 1L year was not all bad. Besides the Sickle Cell Crisis, stereotypes and missing home I met a close friend of mine, Fortune. Fortune was another young black male, he was a 3L so he end up showing me the ropes of law school. Since the first day I met him he has always looked out for me. Fortune was cool too, not as cool as me of course, but still very cool. He believed in me sometimes when I did not even believe in myself. He would always reassure me that I was doing nothing wrong. "Man, little bro do not worry about them, you are going shut everybody up when finals arrive." In a place such as Faulkner, it was felt good to see another young black man offer words of encouragement. Fortune was smart, really smart, almost borderline genius. He does not know this, but he is the one who really showed me how to be myself at Faulkner. That one can wear Jordan's and then put on a tie. That one can like trap music and still have respect for the law. The most important thing he taught me was that we were in this race together and to he was not going to let me quit.

## Campus Police

I was fortunate to never have a run in with the campus police. I have heard about incidents involving some of the other black men on campus; actual friends of mine being harassed by campus security after hours for their student identification cards. The police here are nice guys well towards me at least. 1L year I received a few stares from them as well, but that is it. The security officers liked my car and with my distinct look it was no question I was a student here. When the officers did stop me on campus it was to ask me questions and compliment my car.

## Hunger Games

I referred to law school as the Hunger Games and it really is. If you have not seen the Hunger Games (what planet have you been on) it is a movie where people are in competition to see who can survive in a manmade arena the longest without getting killed. I had a few tricks up my sleeve. I had heard about the deceit and betrayal in law school from upper level law students assigned to us called Dean Fellows. My plan was to sit back, do my own thing and watch the Hunger Games play out in front of me. Law school is very competitive a certain amount of people have to get kicked out after the first year. The Dean Fellows warned us about how conniving and ruthless students can be when trying to secure their spot for class rankings. Between their advice and what Fortune had told me I did not trust anyone.

## Hot Seat

The first time I ever was called on to brief a case was in Torts. This was the longest seven minutes of my life and I will never forget the case I was called to brief until the day I die. Garrett v. Dailey. I was about two months into law school. I found myself reading for many hours at night to get ready for classes the next day. Luckily, I read

this case the night before and made great notes. As the class was about half way finished the Torts teacher looked down on her paper and said "Ralston Jarrett?"
My heart stopped, I stood up nervously paper in hand and she said "So, what happened in Garrett v. Dailey?"
My heart was pounding. "Umm... Well... Dailey a five-year-old boy moved a chair from under Ms. Garrett as she was sitting down and she hurt herself. She then asked "What was the issue here, Mr. Jarrett?"
Uncertain if this was what she is looking for I reply "the issue is whether a battery occurred?"
"Okay" she replies and "What did the court find?" I answered "The court found that a battery can only occur if Garrett acted with substantial certainty that his actions would cause harm to Ms. Garrett?" It's a five second pause. She looked at me, I looked back at her. She nodded her head in approval of my response and said "Good Job, Mr. Jarrett." A sigh of relief for me, I sit down in my seat and thanked God that I did that homework last night. People in the class came up to me afterwards and told me I had done a good job briefing the case. I played it off like it was no big deal, but I was a nervous wreck and glad I had survived.

## Speaking Latin

Learning the law was like learning a new language. You had to study it, master it, and interpret it well enough to recite it back when asked. Many legal terms come from Latin origins so I was learning words like "Res Ipsa Loquitor " " Habeas corpus" " mens rea". For a kid like me who had never spoken in front of more than seven or eight people at a time, briefing my first case in front of my entire law school class was a big deal for me. To read something is one thing, but to read, understand and be able to deliver it back was another thing. I had gotten my professor's approval and my classmates approval and this was a major milestone for me during my 1L year.

## Forming a Team

About halfway through my first semester of 1L year I did not know if I was going to make it; my health was not great and I was always tired. There would be days where I would read for hours and I would still be totally lost and confused during the class lectures. One day while attending the after-school tutoring the school offers I met a young lady who would change my life.

In walked Shenika (a very dear friend of mine now) and she is in there answering a ton of questions and getting the review practice questions correct. I remember her even arguing with the professor on why her answer was right and his was wrong. I was amazed, whoever this young lady was I had to affiliate myself with her, because if I had any chance of making it out of here I needed her help.

The review session ended and we were walking to our cars. I stopped Shenika as she was putting her books in her trunk. I walked over introduced myself and then told her I was having a rough time with the material and was wondering if she would she help me. Ever since that day she has also been one my best friends from law school. While I may not have been very book smart, being wise and street smart definitely got me throughout law school. If one wants to become a drug dealer what does he have to do? Affiliate with someone who deals in those kinds of goods. If one wants to become a politician, what does she have to do? Affiliate with politicians. So, in my case if I had wanted to become a good law student, I had to affiliate with someone who was a good law student. This worked because Shenika's work ethic motivated me and allowed me to put the necessary time and concertation I would need to complete my first year in law school.

## Finals Time

Finals time arrived for us and Shenika and Akeisha (another bright young lady who I had met through Shenika) were getting prepared. Shenika, Akeisha, and I were putting in very long hours at the library and when I was not there Shenika would call and make sure I was doing something pertaining to school.

The first final arrived and it was a lot of pressure. You get only four hours to show the professor everything you have learned in the whole semester. I got to school that morning butterflies in my stomach. My adrenaline is rushing and I am prepared, but I did not get to complete the final. I made the most common rookie law student mistake I spent too much time on the first essay trying to make it sound really good and not enough time on the second essay. Since the essays were weighed equally this hurt my grade severely. I went home and took a nap because the next test was Civil Procedure and I had to do well. The trio (Shenika, Akeisha and I) were putting in long hours, leaving the library close to midnight and the night before the Civil Procedure exam guess what happen? Here comes my Sickle Cell reminding me of its relevance because I had been doing so well with my health the previous weeks. I go in the hospital the night before the test. Dehydration and stress had bought this crisis on.

Luckily, it was only a one day stay. However, I made the worst mistake of my law school career. That night the Dean called me on the telephone to check on me. He asked Would I be able to take the upcoming test Monday and if not they could rearrange it for me to take at a later time. I foolishly told him; I was okay and I would be fine to take it Monday. This was a bad idea. I was on pain medication all day Saturday then I got up Sunday to study for a few hours and went in Monday morning to take the Foundations of Law Exam. I later find out that I failed. This would be the first and only class in law school I failed, I was not adequately prepared like I should have been.

My first law school grade ever was an F. If I did not already feel unfit and unsure I belonged here, this confirmed it. I wanted to quit and act like this had never happened. The rest of the grades came in and they were C's which would have been okay if it had not been before the F I received in the Foundations of Law course. After having my Christmas ruined, I was called into the Academic Dean's Office and put on notice that I was at risk of failing out. They gave me the option to enroll again or to drop out.

After receiving grades, I went to a few of my professors and one of them told me that law school was not for everyone. Although he was right, that was not what I needed to hear at the time. I went to the Torts Professor's office and she looked over my test with me and saw that my writing was good I had just simply run out of time.

But she encouraged me to stay, she reminded me of the case I had brief for her a few weeks ago and told me that she saw something in me that day and to not let one bad grade discourage me.

My Torts Professor was one of the few women professors I had during my first year. Women are natural nurtures and she gave me exactly what I needed at that time, reassurance. I went home and thought about what she and everyone else had said. I love basketball so I would often find myself using basketball analogies throughout law school. I thought about quitting then I said to myself would Michael Jordan quit during half time if he was down by a few points? No, it's a whole second half to be played. So, I walked back in the school the next day and looked the two Deans in their eyes and told them I was staying. That was the best decision I had ever made in my life.

# Chapter 13

## SECOND SEMESTER OF 1L YEAR

### The List

A few days before we were to return to school from Christmas Break, an email was sent to the entire school which had the names of everyone in danger of being academically dismissed. Apparently, someone in the office made the list and I am assuming was trying to send it to the Deans and Faculty, but accidentally sent it to everyone. The list had about 20 names on it including my name and the grade point averages of each individual. As we get back to school people are talking about the list. I heard that people were even making bets on who was going to be here next year and who was going to get kicked out. This is a prime example of how cruel people in law school can be, people laughing and entertained by other peoples' misfortune. This played a role in my success being that I had people counting me out, I used this as fuel to strive even harder second semester.

### Down by 10 in the 4th Quarter

The second half of my 1L year was the hardest I have ever worked in school and the hardest I tried to stay healthy and out of the hospital. As I mentioned earlier, I was always smart. Back in college I could study for the test the night before and still get a decent grade for the course. Law school was different. Law school will make even smart people feel dumb. I knew coming back from Christmas Break that it was game time. I knew this was the semester I was going to be either a law school graduate or a law school dropout, so I was ready to give it my all. From the beginning, I approached my classes in a different way. There were three things that I did differently this semester that I know saved my law school career and saved me from getting kicked out that I would like to share with other upcoming scholars.

The three things I did were study more, made my own outlines, and the most important thing were the newly discovered Supplemental Books that helped me simplify the law. I changed my mindset, I was going to give law school everything I had. If the average law student was in the library for 4 hours I am going to do 6 hours, if I saw someone in there for 6 I would 8 hours. If they wanted me out, they would have to out work me. This is the mindset I had the entire semester. Another thing I changed were my studying habits. Not knowing the intensity of law school when I first arrived I was trying to live a normal life. I was not studying, barely briefing cases, and studying at home with many distractions. I went and purchased a laptop and would takes various notes on my computer during classes. This helped by the end of the semester I had an outline for every class that I had personally written, now when finals were near I would not be learning the material for the first time, but just remembering what I had already written.

## Supplements Are Your Best Friends

As I said before, I found the Supplemental Law Books to be very helpful. One day while walking in the library I found a book that broke down the law very simplistically. I said to myself "A Short and Happy Guide to Torts? Hmm. I think I will read it. I loved it, it was such a breeze to read. Sometimes, the cases we read are hundreds of years old, making them very difficult to understand at times. The Black Letter Law was what the professors wanted and I did not have to read the lengthy cases in order to find it. I went home and got onto a book website and ordered all the supplements that were highly rated. Every semester since, I always purchase supplements for each class. I eventually had a bookcase full and earned the nickname the "Supplement King."

My mentor (Fortune) broke law school to me down like this. It is a competition, a marathon. You do not have to be first all the time, you just have to finish. The way law school is you just have to beat out about 6 people after that it does not matter. The reason for this? Many tests and studies have shown correlation between the passing of the bar and the first year grade point average of a law student. So, from this point on I had a killer instinct. It was not in my nature to sabotage anyone, as I was far too kind with a big conscience, but if they wanted me out of here they were going to have to out work me. I ended the first semester with a 1.46 grade point average. A 1.67 was needed to have a chance to come back and a 2.0 was needed in order to be in good standing. Meaning I needed around a 2.0 in order to not get academically dismissed and a 2.54 in order to be in academic good standing. So, I did what any good student facing academic dismissal would do. I went into beast mode. I thought about the consequences. Do you really want to go home after only one year of law school? Do you really want to go home and explain to everyone how you were not good enough to stay in law school? Do you really want to move back in with your parents? I went to work. I would go to every tutoring session offered, I would go to the library for hours on top of hours. I would keep supplements with me memorizing Black Letter Law every chance I got, I made law school my entire life and not just a part of it.

## Staying Healthy

Around this time, I start taking better care of myself. I worked harder but I knew I did not have the time to get sick this semester. A Sickle Cell Crisis at that point could have cost me my entire career. Sports drinks were my favorite, especially Gatorade. I would always keep tons of water and sports drinks in the school's fridge to avoid dehydration. My most painful Sickle Cell Crisis have come from being dehydrated, therefore sports drinks were crucial to my health. My stress levels were at a maximum so I had to eat right and take care of myself. Another thing I discovered was oxygen. Right before law school my girlfriend was complaining about my snoring at night while we were sleeping. So, I went to a Pulmonologist and discovered that I stop breathing in my sleep which was the reason my snoring was so loud. I was given a machine that provides oxygen while sleeping to reduce my snoring. It was later that I found out that not only did it actually stop my snoring, but it also helped with my Sickle Cell Crises. Since a youth, I would always get a crisis while I was sleeping. I would be in so much pain that it would wake me out of my sleep. Since I was willing to do whatever it took to stay healthy, I started sleeping with the machine. This made me feel much better and the number of crises I got per month significantly dropped from once a week to once a month, or sometimes none. This was a major milestone I discovered with the hydration from water and sports drinks, getting enough sleep, eating well, and my newly discovered oxygen I felt better than I had in a long time.

I was feeling better, which allowed me to study more. On Saturdays, instead of going to the movies or hanging out with my girlfriend Monica all weekend I would go to the library. I would then come home and take her to a movie or out to a nice restaurant. I never slept in on Sunday mornings like her so I would either go get waffle house for her (which she loved) or I would wake up and cook breakfast. Not cereal, but a real breakfast her favorite: salmon patties, bacon, eggs, grits and home fries. I would be exhausted after this, but it was just my way of showing her that I appreciated all that she had done for me. After breakfast and a little down time, I was right back in the library.

Around this time, I had started to get the hang of law school. One day I had a Crisis and still went to class, but I was late. My Legal Writing teacher let me have it. I walked in and she stopped and asked me "Did I think I could just come when I feel like it?" I said "no" and she docked a few points off from me, but it was fine. She did not know I was feeling terrible on the inside that day because I had a Crisis a few hours before, and in fact she was right I was late. Even if I was sick, I should have been on time or not have come to class that day. Law school often showed tough love at times.

## Proving Myself

The semester was almost done and it was time for Oral Arguments. The class was Legal Research and Writing and it was taught by my favorite Professor. I have a lot of respect for her because I would come to this woman's office about three times a week, if I did not understand something and she never turned me away. Down the line, she told me she believed in me and could not deny the determination I had and loved how my writing gradually improved since she began teaching me. She even apologized for riding me in front of everyone the day I came in late.

Practice rounds for Oral Arguments had arrived. We got our case and we were told to go home and prepare. I did not take the task seriously. I was not prepared, I did terrible and my opponent Matt ate me alive. Not only did he eat me alive, the judges, my Legal Writing Professor and her colleagues let me have it. I forgot a courtroom rule and got scolded for it. On top of that, I was embarrassed because I did not know the facts of my case. I called my professor that night and she gave me the some of the best advice ever when it comes to litigation, "Know the facts of your case." I took that advice and ran with it. The next week we had graded rounds and I needed the best possible grade in order to get off academic probation. For a week I ate with that case, I slept with that case, I went to the bathroom with that case I made sure I memorized as many facts as possible from that case to make a valid argument for my graded round. After that I wrote an opening and memorized it. Shenika and Akeisha listened to it, gave a few pointers and my boy Quinton gave me some advice about confidence and owning the courtroom when you walk in.

The day came along and I was prepared. I went against a good friend of mine, but as far as I was concerned from 4:00pm to 4:30pm that day, I did not have any friends. We were two dogs on the field, fighting for the last bone and I needed that bone more than she did. To make matters worse the court room was packed.

My Legal Writing Professor walked in, the fake bailiff yelled "All Rise" and she saw the large crowd and asked if we would like her to clear the courtroom, I said "No Your Honor". In my head, I was thinking *No this is my show, the Ralston show for the next 12 minutes I want them to see this.* I do not remember much after that. I went in beast mode. I went all in, throwing out arguments and rebuttals left and right. I held nothing back this was my grade and I wanted to show my professor and the rest of the school I deserved to be here. I was not here because I was Black, I was not here because my parents were rich, I was here because I deserved to be here.

After the arguments was over my professor had the biggest smile on her face she was trying to hide it. The crowd was also smirking in disbelief from what I had just done. After my professor gave constructive criticism on how to improve, I was greeted with many hugs and high fives. I exited the courtroom that day a winner and I end up getting a decent grade in my Legal, Research and Writing class. From my argument, I did receive a good grade, but more importantly, I earned my respect around the school. It was not long before the word had gotten around that Ralston had shocked the entire court room with his oral argument. It was that moment when my classmates gained a new-found respect for me. I had shown them what I knew all along. I am more than my outer appearance and I deserved to be here.

As finals approached this time, I was prepared physically and mentally. I walked in each final and wrote down everything I remembered from those late-night sessions in the library, from all the supplements I read, the notes I had taken in class and wrote it just as how my Legal Writing Professor had taught me. Walking out of my last final I felt nervous. I had given my all, but I wondered would that be good enough? As a little boy, I must have played in over 100 basketball games whether recreational or pickup and I did not mind losing. What would often haunt me is when I would lose and I knew deep down inside that I could have played a little better, ran a little faster, grabbed a few more rebounds, shot a few more jump shots, those were the toughest loses. I did not mind losing as much when I gave it my all and still came up short. That is how it was with my first year of law, after my last final of my 1L year I knew I had left it all in that classroom and I had nothing to be ashamed about.

It was two weeks of torturous waiting, I got a notification on my phone from one of my classmates "Constitutional Law is up" I said a prayer and check it I made a C. I was happy but I needed more for that 2.5. The next few days they roll in, Property grade C, Legal Research and Writing Course C+ , Civil Procedure B and last Contracts B. I was still disappointed I did not get the 2.54 I needed, but I did get a 2.35 enough to be asked back. I was academically dismissed from law school, but able to come back on the second chance program where I enrolled in summer classes.

My advice to Jordan and Nicholas is to keep pushing, 1L year is always the worst. Between being homesick, the outside distractions going on back home and the pressure to do well; it can get intense. The outside world is your enemy first year. The distractions will destroy you, if you let them. This will have to be the most selfish year of your life. You will need to learn how to say "no" to family members, friends, and anything that can potentially take time away from you studying. You will have stepped into mental boot camp. The law school wants to weed out the weak right now. I suggest study groups; a study group is always good, the smaller the better. Its best to get someone you feel is smarter than you this will push you to do better. I urge Jordan and Nicholas not to solely rely on other people's outlines, half of the learning from an outline is writing it out on your own. Supplements are highly recommended and contributed to a lot of my success in law school.

For Nicholas, I just advise him to stay as healthy as possible. No one will ever understand how it feels to go to class after or even during a Sickle Cell Crisis. What I want Nicholas to do is to stay hydrated and as stress free as possible. Also, let the staff know what is going on with you. I am very private with my Sickle Cell but I imagine things would have been easier if people had known. The hard part for me was digging myself out of the hole from my low first semester grades. If they both can have a good first semester, then the second semester will not be as hard. As far as for people and their acceptance of you some people will like you, others will not. This is law school - We are not here to make friends, find a few decent people and study with them, exchange numbers in case the other misses a class or notes need to be exchanged.

# Chapter 14

## NEW FOUND FAME

When I got back home to Columbus after my 1L year things had changed drastically. Good news travels fast. When you are doing something positive people always want to associate themselves with you. This was a big change for me since I am a private person. Coming home from law school I was a hometown hero. They say if you are a hero you have to deny being a hero or otherwise you are a jerk. So, I always acted modest anytime someone bought up law school. But, unfortunately, with success comes jealousy and hate. While I will always remain true to my friends before law school. After the word got back around I was in law school, people started coming in to my life by the dozens. As I am seeing now when you are doing well people want to praise and associate themselves with you. Even if they played no part in the success. Coming home most of my close friends still treated me the same. But, it was other people who I noticed a change in after my return.

My family even felt the change in people. My dad was even acting a little different, I later found out a friend of his had a family member go to law school and flunked out. My dad's friend told him how hard it was. Until this point, I do not think he understood the difficulty I was facing. Until, I got back my father never really acknowledged my accomplishment. Now, my mom on the other hand was proud of me just for not giving up and overcoming everything. My sister was my number one supporter bragging to anyone who would listen to her talk about her brother being in law school. Monica had people telling her how lucky she was to have a man who was about to be a lawyer. I never thought that me going to school would have such an effect on my life. When you are in law school people respect you, they always would say "that's my lawyer" or "I may need you in the future."

## Peanut

I remember seeing some childhood friends when I was home for a few days immediately after finishing my 1L year. I had stopped at the local gas station before getting back on the road to Montgomery and ran into them. It had been a while since I had seen them but we had all grown up together and been knowing each other since the age of 12. I got out the car to pump my gas and they came up with the biggest smiles on their faces. Like "Oh shit "What up, Peanut? Peanut then came back home!" Peanut was a nickname my sister had given to me at the age of seven because of my small head. It was a cool nick name that I went by for years until I got to high school. Telling someone my name was Peanut was easier than trying to tell them my name was Ralston and cringing at them butcher the pronunciation. So, that is what I went by. But over the years I felt like I had outgrown the nickname and I hated when anyone else besides my sister would call me that. I said "Ralston!" and they looked at me in confusion. I said "its Ralston now man, don't call me Peanut" and smiled at them, we all laughed about it then one of them said "Man, I know you as Peanut I don't care how big of a lawyer you become, I'm a call you Peanut." We all laughed again about it and now they call me Ralston or they will see me and say "What up Peanut! I mean Ralston!' just to give me a hard time. I had hope not to come off as arrogant or cocky, but I felt like law school had changed me and matured me and I just did not want to be called by my childhood nickname anymore.

Aside from my neighborhood friends, everyone else seemed to be extra courteous to me all of a sudden. When people think, they may need you, they watch out for you. They check on you more often, they try to stay in your good graces. Law school meant respect and I loved it. Women who would not give me the time of day before, were in my inboxes on social media. I would go out to the clubs and would not have to reach in my pocket for anything. Law school bought me power and respect. Power and respect that I did not have before.

## Toll on my body

Law school really put a toll on my body. It is probably one of the most stressful things a person can do. Unfortunately for me, Sickle Cell and stress from law school did not go together very well. While my classmates would often go to the gym to relieve their stress I could not do this and had to find other alternative methods. I personally would like to go to the shooting range, cooking and even sex if Monica was up for it. But even with sex I would still have to be careful since it is physical activity. I have had many Sickle Cell Crises after having sexual intercourse. Ironically, I had to be extremely cautious on the way I would deal with my stress during the three most stressful years of my life.

As I mentioned earlier and as crazy as this may still sound I never would tell people I had Sickle Cell. As a kid, you do not want to be different. Kids being kids would often ask me why my eyes were yellow. (yellow eyes are symptoms of Sickle Cell) and I probably said something smart back. But that is how I learned to think quick on my feet. If someone came up being mean I could not cry, I had to come right back with an insult. "Why are your eyes yellow?" "Why are your shoes so dirty?" "Why are your eyes so cocked?" They probably did not mean any harm, but believe it or not since my dad was in the military I would often make friends by talking smack back to people who would mess with me. Kids can be cruel; I think that is why I am so secluded with my illness even as an adult.

Unless you are a close friend of mine you would never know about my illness, many people still do not know. In my experience, people do not really care that you have Sickle Cell they just want to be nosey and in your personal business. For the most part I did a really good job maintaining my health in my three years here I think I may have been hospitalized only four or five times. One might be saying that is not good, but for the type of stress and adversity I was facing that is very good! After a while going to the hospital did not even bother me, a Crisis was a regular thing to me. Similar to how most people get their teeth cleaned twice a year, I knew I would be in the hospital. It did not even phase me, I started to look at it as paying dues for the profession I had chosen. After I would get a blood transfusion and some pain medication I would feel like a brand-new man. Nurses would come in my room at 3:00am to give me pain medication I would be up doing multiple choice questions with an IV hanging out my hand. The doctors would hold a big meeting and would come to my room in a group and expect to see a broken and distraught guy, I would be up eating breakfast listening to lecture videos asking them could I go home.

Besides the Sickle Cell, law school also affected my vision. After my 1L year I made an appointment to see the eye doctor because I had noticed my vision had gotten drastically worse while driving. Many of my classmates complained about the same thing happening to them. We figured the mass amounts of reading we did 1L year destroyed our vision. My hair was also starting to gray. I had never had a gray hair in my head until 1L year. Eventually the gray went away, but I thought my locs were going to turn gray for a while. I developed a slight cause of insomnia. I was not sleeping my first year I would take three hour naps, maybe another two-hour nap if I was lucky but it was no more sleeping in for eight or more hours. This is something I still suffer with even as a 3L. Now I have to constantly take sleeping pills just to put my mind at rest some nights. The feeling of competitiveness that you must always be working because there is someone out there studying more than you can be a good thing, but also a bad thing. This feeling never allows me to rest because on down time I feel like I should be doing something to academically improve myself. In law school, there should never be a time when you have no work to do it is always something to be done.

My doctor tried to put me on medication to help with my Sickle Cell Crisis. I did not see a difference so I discontinued my use. The side effects were greater than the potential benefits, one being infertility.

A fear of dying before being able to reproduce was always a big fear of mine. With the life expectancy rate of a person with Sickle Cell being about half of a normal person I always thought that I would have children at a young age, so I would be able to be around them while they were growing up. Sometimes I resent coming to law school because with the constant pain crisis I thought I was somehow speeding up my demise from all of the stress I was incurring. There are many factors and sacrifices that come with law school.

My advice to Jordan and Nicholas is to be prepared for the people around them to start to change, especially the ones back home when they find out you came to law school. Take care of yourself and keep stress to a minimum especially Nicholas. It would be impossible to study twenty-four hours a day so find a good stress reliever that will keep stress levels down. Make constant doctor's appointments with a physician one or twice a semester. Purchase reading glasses as your eyes will be strained from the excess amount of reading that will have to be done. For Nicholas, take your medicine everyday if you feel it helps with your health. Nicholas has a daughter already so the side effects may not scare him away as it did for me. Finally, get lots of rest as much as possible.

# Chapter 15

## MATURING

Law school changed me. Before law school the only time, I would wear glasses is to look cool. After my 1L year I could barely see without them. I eventually went to see an optometrist and got glasses. He confirmed this was common with medical and law students due to the constant strain on the eyes from reading as my classmates and I had suspected. I found myself dressing differently. Those Jordan's I owned turned into dress shoes. The white tee shirts turned into dress shirts and my cargo shorts turned into dress slacks. Going to the mall was different. Instead of going to the sneaker store first I was going to grownup stores, the stores I hated to go in as a youth when my mom would take me before a family wedding or funeral. But my love for sneakers, gave me the best of both worlds, it would just depend on how I would feel that day. Somedays I would still wear Jordan's and a tee shirt. I was talking differently not using as much profanity, the "what up bruh" turned into "what up bro". I thought about things before actually saying them. I was finally able to get rid of my street mentality, I did not feel like a target here as I often felt back home. Law school effects everyone differently, my change that I made after coming was for the better.

My parents even said they noticed me maturing. I once read only a fool does not change. If you are in a new environment you are going to eventually adapt to that new environment in order to survive. When in Rome, do as the Romans right? I did not enjoy watching television as much anymore. Even when I did I found myself watching Court TV, Judge Judy, the People's Court, and especially Judge Mathis. Law school had changed my brain. For fun I would actually watch the case, hear the facts, and try to guess the correct law before the verdict was held for either the plaintiff or defendant. Wheel of fortune, also became a favorite of mine, it got to a point where my family did not even enjoying playing with me anymore, because I would always get the puzzle right. Law school had taken my brain and tuned it up really well. I was doing things I did not know I was mentally capable of doing. This was a whole new experience for me while I did not want to forget where I came from I eventually had to grow up and drop that street mentality once and for all. I had to teach myself that it was okay to get smarter, it was okay to want better, it was okay to remove people from my life, it was okay to change and that anyone who loved me would understand. Many friends noticed my growth after returning home, -some stood around for it, while others wanted no part of my new-found intellect.

My advice to Jordan and Nicholas here would be to be prepared for the change law school brings along. Law school changes everything about you from the way you dress to the way you think and all of your interests. My friends and I would always joke that the Professors had took out each one of our brains while we were sleep and re-programmed them to think like them. This is exactly what it felt like. After my first year of law school I was never the same. I was 24 going on 25 so I had matured a lot. Changing my environment allowed me to get rid of some of the street mentality I had picked up since the attempted robbery. In Montgomery, I did not have to watch my back, I felt safe. I felt like I was able to let my guard down without anything bad happening to me. Here the worst thing that could possibly happen to me is me getting called on in class and not being prepared. While back home in Columbus, I constantly lived in fear of getting shot, robbed, jumped etc... I think Nicholas will really enjoy law school. Sometimes it is not you that got in trouble, it was the environment you are in that will force you to do something you would not have done if you were somewhere else. Law school definitely will change both Jordan and Nicholas it will be a brand-new experience for them that will be very beneficial for the both of them.

# Chapter 16

## SECOND YEAR OF LAW SCHOOL

I will never forget the first day of my 2L year. I was in class and the Professor was going over the syllabus. Half of the class is paying attention and the other half is not, the Professor who happened to be an older white female dropped her folders. Now while I admit I was not paying attention either, but my mother always told me to treat a woman how I would want someone to treat her. So after I saw no one was going to pick the folders she had dropped, I stood up and walked towards her she continued to talk while keeping a close eye on me. As I got closer everyone is looking up like what is Ralston doing? As I approached her she tensed up and said "Yes?" I approached her and said "Oh nothing, just getting your folders for you!" Everyone smiled and kind of laughed, that day I think a lot of people learned who I truly was as a person. There was no reason to fear me I was a kind genuine soul with a smile that could light up the room. From that day on the Professor would smile every time she would see me and the rest of the class took a liking toward me as well.

Now that I was a 2L, I knew what to expect and was happy to have been able to return. Toward the end of the summer of my 1L year rumors that we would have an African American Professor next year started to circulate. As you can imagine the minority students were happy. I remember walking into my Criminal Procedure class the first week of 2L year and seeing him for the first time. I along with the rest of my classmates were thinking this class should be fun and interesting especially with a Black law professor. I walked in the first day looking at my other colleagues; we are all smiling giving each other high fives. "Nigga we made it!" Devon said to me right before he slapped me five. It was not that we did not like our other professors, but when you see someone who looks like you in a position you want to be in one day, it is a good feeling.

Those smiles were instantly wiped off of our faces the minute class started. The way this guy read the syllabus we knew he meant business and his class would be no walk in the park. As the semester went on we all grew a respect for him, besides his strict classroom rules which included no one being able to come in late or leave to use the bathroom (which were rare rules for upper level law students) the guy knew his material, and made me a better law student with his teaching methods. Contrary to our initial thoughts of him being this cool, savvy, easy going professor he was tough as nails. If anything he was a little harder on the minority students than others.

2L year is also when I met another one of my close friends at law school. Her name was Tiffany and she was from Georgia as well so that was how we bonded. Tiffany was from Atlanta about 90 minutes north of Columbus. We both were in the same boat taking a few classes over after a rough start during our 1L year. It is ironic that we both had trouble in the same classes but did well in our second semesters. We had every class together that semester so I guess meeting and becoming friends was inevitable. Her boyfriend was from Columbus and we would often talk about how much better we both liked Columbus better than Montgomery. It is always cool to have a good, genuine friend in law school in case you are running late and need them to hold on to the attendance sheet until you arrive or just someone to get notes for you on days you cannot attend class.

The year started off great besides those few classes I had to repeat because of the horrific first semester; Things were starting to look up, I had new friends, new studying approaches and I was just glad to be there and not back home in Columbus (as the guy who had been dismissed from law school). My friend Rachel who I went to Columbus State with joined me at Faulkner this year as well. We had studied for the LSAT together and I promised to look out for her at Faulkner if she was accepted. Unfortunately, my law school best friend Stephen from 1L year did not return. Stephen was homesick. His wife was in medical school back in Texas and he had no family here. Every time he wanted to go home he would have to get on a plane. Being law students we do not have the time or money for either. We talked and I tried to get him to return, but I completely understood when he did not. I had Monica with me to not make me feel so alone and my immediately family was 90 miles away from me if I needed them but I can imagine how rough it can be all alone in a strange city away from your loved ones. Luckily, I still had my good friend Shenika, while Akeisha had transferred to the University of Alabama's law school. 2L year, was when I got involved with the school more and also the year I got to go to court and view real lawyers in action. I had been assigned to go to Family Court in Montgomery.

Many people do not know that I wanted to do Juvenile Criminal Defense when I first started law school. I met a District Attorney in Montgomery that allowed me to shadow her for a few weeks. After the first day, I knew I did not want to do Juvenile Defense anymore. As a law student, we are told not to take our work home, which means do not get to emotionally attached to a client. As much as I wanted to remain unattached I could not. What I saw in that court room made me feel bad for days. The court handled juvenile delinquents, I saw many young men with lots of potential and no guidance. The sad thing about this is that the majority of them all had two things in common: one they were young and Black and two they grew up in single mother homes. I do not have any children but I thought *what if this was my son?* It saddened me the judge is naming all of these serious offenses, burglary, theft of a vehicle, possession of a gun during the commission of a crime and in my head I am thinking this little pipsqueak did all of that? I would take my belt off right now if I was his father. I went to a few more cases just to see how the proceedings went, but I knew I was not cut out for juvenile cases.

## No Place for the Weak

My 2L year was also the first time I was yelled at by a judge. I had asked the retired judge who was my criminal law teacher a question on how the structure of her final exam would be. She said she would probably know the next class period because she had not written the exam yet. With me being a repeat student of the course I was not afraid to ask a question because my first-year jitters were over. The next class approached and I walked in with my normal jolly attitude with some Jordan's on, a baseball cap (like I did on most days unless I had to go to court). The judge was taking questions and asks the class did they have any questions. No one raised their hand. I raised my hand and asked the judge about the structure of the exam again thinking she had probably just forgotten I had asked. She must not have been in a good mood because she went in angry judge mode quick. She said in a mean Judge Judy voice "take your cap off, while you are talking to me!" I felt my stomach go in knots. I am thinking *is she a Boston Red Sox's fan or something, it is a New York Yankees hat.* But as I continue to look at her I realized she was not joking so I started to walk out of the classroom, but instead I just took the hat off like she asked. The whole room went quiet because the reaction was so unprovoked. I had asked her plenty of questions with my hat on and she had never said anything about it. This was the last day in the semester before break and now she decided to yell at me? She asked me to restate my question again. I said nothing. I am a nice funny guy who rarely blows my cool, so I knew it was best for me to sit there and say nothing. I learned a long time ago especially with being a young Black male, sometimes it is better to just let it go. Every battle does not have to be fought, pick and choose which ones to fight wisely. Nothing good would have come from me saying anything at that point. I would have been criticized for being an angry, thug, who cursed out the judge, so I simply held my tongue. To show the class it did not phase me, I kind of just laughed it off and started back taking notes in my computer like it did not bother me, but it did deep down inside.

I looked up and the new incoming 1L's are laughing. I mean really laughing to the point were they are turning red. It was funny to them, I took offense because I was really asking for the classes benefit. If I was a different kind of guy I could have just went up to her and asked her myself what was the format of the test and kept the information a secret. I just did not like the double standards going on that I was dealing with not only then but my entire life. Can we imagine if those roles were reversed and I a young, Black, dread head, Jordan wearing, student had said something disrespectful to an elderly white woman? Unprovoked! The result would not have been laughter but would have been fear. "OMG, what is wrong with that black guy! He is such a thug." He does not have to talk to her like that, I am going to tell Administration." But this was not my first rodeo, I knew people were expecting me to act a certain way so I did not give them the satisfaction. I did go to her office afterwards and to my surprise she was nice about the situation. I walked in looking for her to be angry so I could get angry but she was not.

I will never forget when I asked her what was the deal with her and the fiasco. She looked at me so nonchalantly and said "don't take it personal, you got to have tough skin in this business." She told me the format of the test and left. I sat outside her office flabbergasted. Don't take it personal?! You yell at me and embarrass me in front of the whole class and say do not take it personal? I took it very personal. I thought to myself *if I was a young white male with an Auburn hat on whose parents were lawyers would she have talked to me like that?* Probably not. Out of all the students in the class to go haywire on you chose me? I just did not understand because it was so unprovoked. If I had come in late I would have expected it, if I had been disrupting class I would have expected it. I got yelled at for no reason, but I want to thank the judge for that tough love, when I do become a lawyer I will have tough skin. While I was angry for the rest of the day I eventually had gotten over it. Besides her and my Legal Writing Professor, all of my professors had been nice and welcoming towards me. But in practice I am sure not every judge will be kind. Now I am prepared to take the criticism and unprovoked verbal attacks from authority figures in my profession without being distraught -thanks to the judge.

## Black Law Students Association

2L year I joined the Black Law Student's Association (BLSA) on campus. BLSA is a major organization that allows for black students on campus to meet once a month and discuss things. This is where I was able to network with other Black students even the ones I was avoiding after I heard they were spreading those rumors about me last year. BLSA was great. We are the Faulkner chapter, but they have the organization at many other law schools across the country. BLSA was not only a way to socialize with my peers, they were really there to help the 1L students stay on track. They are also involved in many school functions and organize many events in the community. I got really involved with BLSA and would help out the 1L students with whatever they needed. I would help them just as Fortune had helped me during my first year.

## Giving Back

I took Rachel under my wing after she got here. While I had graduated a year before her at Columbus State, Rachel would often call me during my 1L year to check on me and offer words of encouragement. It felt good having someone from my undergraduate university here at the law school with me. I promised that I would show her the ropes and tell her all of the things I did wrong in order to prevent her from making some of the same mistakes I had made. Since Faulkner remade me take a few courses from my first semester after not getting the 2.0 GPA Rachel and I would often study together. She adjusted to the law school life very well, most people do not. I think I scared her to death when she would call me during my first year and ask what I was doing and I would always say, "I am in the library".

As the semester continued and finals wrap up, Rachel called me and asked me to help her prepare for the Annual 1L year mock trial event Jones offered every year. I was still being cocky from what I had learned during my 1L year doing trials, so I agreed to help. The event is held every year and it allowed first year law students to argue in the school's courtroom. The winner received a trophy and bragging rights. The professors are present and they scout to see who they want for the school's trial team.

The trial team is composed of the best advocates at Faulkner and established to compete against other law schools around the country. A few days before Rachel was to go in the 1L competition she had come over to show me what she had prepared for the competition. Monica and I were eating dinner, she came and ate with us and then we got to it. It started off horrible. Rachel was as stiff as a board, her tone was boring, and she could not stop saying "umm".

But fortunately, Rachel was a great listener and everything I told her to do she did. I remember I told her "when arguing a case in front of a courtroom, this is your show. If you had a television show would you want people falling asleep or being bored while watching, you? In the courtroom, you have a job and that is to convince the judge or jury that you know what you are talking about and you honestly believe what you are saying." Although I had changed my major in college from theater, I would often find myself acting and giving performances in law school. We stayed up for hours, just writing and rehearsing her case.

When preparing a case, you have to have a theme for the case which is a catch phrase that grabs and holds the attention of the audience. The best advice I could give her is what my Legal Writing Professor told me "know your facts". It is hard teaching someone how to litigate because everyone has what I call their own court room swagger. This cannot be taught you have to find out what works for you the only way to find your swagger is by practicing. I have nice teeth, so I like to smile and interact with the jury to get them to like me,-this works for me. I would get up and show her how I would litigate the facts of this case. Rachel would eventually have to find her own technique. So, a few hours go by and she is still practicing. I was on the couch asleep and Monica who was watching at first had already went to sleep on us a few hours prior. While in and out of sleep I see Rachel in front of my hallway mirror. I would wake up say "do it again" and go back to sleep. I woke back up and one of them came out good, very good. I think I might have said "wow" whatever she did I told her to keep doing it. With her practice and my fine tuning, she had improved drastically. This was at the beginning of the week, by the end of the week she had perfected her swagger and was ready for the competition on Monday.

When Monday arrived, she came in and destroyed the competition. The crowd was in awe and I just sat back in the audience acting in fake disbelief with them like I did not know where she got that court room swagger from. While she did not win the entire competition, she made it to the semi-finals and ended up making the trial team for the school.

## Racism

The second semester of my 2L year approached and things were good. My family would often come visit Monica and I in Montgomery. My friends would often come visit us as well if we could not make it home. Everything was everything. The hurdle to get off academic probation was almost over and I had survived. As soon as things started going well, here comes the racism. The most openly racist thing I have encountered in law school was done by a 1L student from Rachel's incoming class.

I was a 2L at the time. The student who I had seen on campus numerous times and actually spoken to on various occasions had made a post on social media that angered many people. The girl posted a status referring to her disapproval of some black women who she had encountered at a restaurant in Montgomery. She then continued to express her disapproval after a few African Americans at our school told her that it was not fair to generalize an entire race just from the actions of two women she had encountered. The girl instead of retreating, proceeded to emphasize that in her life she has known most black people to be the same, loud, rambunctious, trouble makers like the ones at the restaurant. The finale was when one of her family members who was a member of the Ku Klux Klan (KKK) commented on the status showing his approval of the controversial post. There was an outrage, people at Jones were highly upset.

The Deans were quickly notified of this and from what I heard it was not even an African American who reported her. This post had angered the entire school. The Administration quickly handled it, and eventually the girl who made the post was not seen on campus anymore. My view on Jones changed that day. While some class members who had a voice did not speak on it there were many who did stand up for us and said that this was not right. Racism is very active in the world today but, it is a difference from seeing it on television and when it actually hits close to home. I cannot see how one could be racist toward any one group of people in this profession. Whenever I do become a lawyer, after I take the oath I will fight for each and every client like they are a family member of mine (as I think all lawyers should). But how could one properly do this if they have hatred in their heart toward a certain group of people? A lawyer must be open minded and not generalize or assume anything about anyone.

My advice to Jordan and Nicholas would be to have patience. Things will get better your second year of law school. At first no one liked me, but my second year of law school people eventually came around and started liking me at law school. For Nicholas, I just want to warn him of the intimidation he will put into people here just because he is a young Black male. It is unfortunate but that is how it goes. The truth is some people will not like you just because you are Black. People will think you do not deserve to be here and you only got accepted because you are Black. I hate to be so straight forward, but that is the honest truth. As you can see racism is still very prevalent today -even on our campus. I hope he has more of a relaxed attitude because people will try to get under your skin and push your buttons just to see how you will react. Even with Jordan every fight does not have to be fought sometimes. It is best to just ignore and walk away. I know Nicholas was concerned about the diversity of the school. Our graduating class is 30% Black. There are only eight Black males. There is myself, Reggie, Devon, James, Tyler, Lowell, Joseph, and Quinton. The black women outnumber us tremendously. The group BLSA, I mentioned earlier is a good way to meet people on campus, although they are called Black Law Students Association, you do not have to be Black to be a member. I found it awesome that some members where not Black and the school really embraces the group. Our presence is really felt on campus. When at law school do not be afraid to join these types of groups for networking and do not be afraid to reach out to upper level law students for assistance.

# Chapter 17

## BETRAYAL

Monica and I would attend all social gatherings the school had. I would love to watch her shop for formal dresses for hours in the mall whenever I had a big social event we had to attend. I would always complain and acted like it did not matter which one she picked but deep down I would just be happy she was coming to support me. We attended many social gatherings and I would often introduce her to my Professors and classmates during these events. While the food would be horrible and the event usually a bore it never seemed too bad because she was there. Looking back at it now 2L year was the time I got closer with school but eventually drifted away from Monica without even realizing. I thought we were okay because we would often attend my social events together and would have a blast, but besides that we did not have time for much else. Being on Academic Probation the school required that I pass every class I had to retake or I would be Academically Dismissed. So, to avoid this the long nights at the library begun. Monica started to feel neglected. I could not give her all the time she needed and she told me she wanted a baby. I told her I could not give her a baby right now.

As the weeks went by, I am working harder than ever during my 2L year to get off of Academic Probation. She was happy, I was happy and life was good. One day I took to Birmingham to shop, eat, and do all the things we like to do together. After we got home she received a call from her mother, saying her Grandmother was in the hospital and she had suffered a stroke. She went to Columbus immediately. I wanted to come with her for support, but I could not. Unfortunately, this occurred during midterms and I could not go home with Monica. I did send a care package with lots of food just to express my condolences. When she left that time to go home a little part of our relationship walked out with her.

As, the weeks go by her grandmother got better and recovered fully. I do not know if someone said anything to Monica, but she was just never the same again after the incident. I think guilt came from leaving her family to be with me and pursue her career in Montgomery started to bother her. With me being so busy with school, she started to go to Columbus more often to check on her family.

Monica's Grandmother was starting to get back to normal. I called her grandmother a few times to check on her. A few weeks had gone by and her grandmothers' health seems to be getting better. Monica was still commuting to Columbus, much often than before. I did not think anything of it, I assumed she was handling business, checking on family, and giving me alone time to study. This continued for weeks. Finals arrived I complete my two weeks of intensive studying while she was going back and forth to Columbus. The semester ended well. I kicked ass and was not on Academic Probation anymore.

After finals, I usually take a week off just to relax, catch up on sleep, and hydrate. Monica's birthday was around the corner. I had set up a romantic get a way in Florida for us to celebrate and to show my appreciation I had for her.

The day after my last final, I got a Sickle Cell Crisis. Monica came home hours early to check on me, she then said she had to go to Columbus. This was strange that she wanted to leave after I had finished finals and was free for the weekend. On top of that, I was not feeling good and she knew this. Monica had never left me by myself before during a Crisis. She went to Columbus. I stayed in Montgomery to hydrate and rest. I started feeling better. It was a Friday night, I had just finished my 2L year and I was at home on the couch. So, I drove to Columbus to see my family and to surprise Monica and her grandmother. I get to Columbus about 8:00pm and talk to my parents for a few hours. I was laying down about to go to bed and my friend Tray called and asked me to go to a local night club with him. I told him I was just going to stay home. He asked me again, so I said I would go but only stay for a little while. I called Monica a few times to inform her I was in town. I had gotten some flowers I wanted to give to her grandmother, but she did not respond, (which was unusual of her).

So, Tray and I are out at the night club. I had bought him a drink and I had an orange juice and water in my hand to stay hydrated. We were sitting down at a table waiting for a pool table to get free as midnight approached. Tray and I are talking and I looked to my left and I see a beautiful girl walk in the club. I continue talking to Tray and I am not really paying attention to her because she is with a guy. So, I continued talking. Suddenly the crowd clears and I see the guy and the girl completely now. In the middle of a sentence I just stop talking, my mouth was wide open and Tray looked over. He must have seen the look on my face because he looked at me and asked "You good?" No I was not good, the beautiful girl was Monica and she was with a guy whose name I do not know, but I will refer to as "Little Dude" (a nick name I had given to him because she is taller than him).

I thought she was at home spending time with her grandmother so I am furious. Before Tray could even finish the pronunciation in "good" I am out of my chair. This was the moment Tray transitioned from a casual friend of mine to an honorary family member because as I got up charging toward Monica he was two steps behind me. I grabbed her arm removing her from the club in an angry rage. I asked her what was going on the only thing she could say was "she did not want any drama." I told her to get in the car and let's go home now! She looked me in my eyes and said "no" -I was like get in the car and come home with me now or its over between us. She turned around and walked away from me to go back in the club. My heart stopped, my eyes watered up, my fist clinched. Here comes that street mentality I was trying so hard to stray away from. I turned around I walked to my car and got my pistol out. I thought about it, then put the pistol back in the car, I was not about to throw everything I had worked so hard for down the drain. It is very easy to get into trouble when you let your emotions cloud your common sense, but I knew I was not about to shoot anyone especially over that even though I felt my little heart breaking right at that moment. So, I go back in the club and now I am furious. *You don't want any drama? Well I am about to give you plenty of it.* I am looking for little dude she was with because I want smoke (smoke is street slang for a confrontation). I went back in the club and I scanned people looking for little dude. I felt my phone vibrating, it was Tray trying to make sure I am okay. I spotted her in the corner with this stupid look of guilt on her face, but little dude is nowhere to be found. I am still hot just walking around the club and guess who I run into?

It is Wade! My friend from high school who had stopped the guys from jumping me back in college. He said "What up Ralston?" I instantly smiled and we shook hands. I had not seen Wade in about three years since I went off to law school. As I am writing this memorandum, I am starting to think that this guy may be my guardian angel or something. He always seemed to show up out of nowhere and just at the right times. After I finished talking to Wade, I had calmed down tremendously. I then went and found Tray and told him I was about to leave. He said "I know you in school and you can't do much you want me to handle it?" I told him it is not his fault and left. I just went home. I went home and cried. I do not know if they were tears of anger or sadness, maybe a little bit of both. I called her 10 times just hoping she would realize what she had just done. She did not answer and eventually turned her phone off. I went to sleep. I wanted to wake up and pretend it was just a nightmare. This could not be true, my best friend would never do this to me, my best friend would not ruin our friendship and betray me like this.

I logged on to social media and she had posted a picture. I will never forget the post because the caption cut through my heart like a bullet. It read "my ex asked me where I'm going I said on to better things."

I went the whole weekend acting like nothing bothered me, but deep down I was an emotional wreck. This cannot be true, Tray called me to check on me and see how I was doing. He said Little Dude looked like he wanted to try something as I was pulling Monica out the club and he was ready for whatever I wanted to do. I thanked him but it was no need to retaliate. My beef was not with the guy it was with her. I just wanted smoke with him that night because I did not know how to direct my anger and I could not hit her. I am just glad he did not come outside when I went back to the car to retrieve my pistol.

I went back to Montgomery. I had to get out of Columbus before I got into some serious trouble.

The weekend went by and Monica called to tell me that she was not in love with me anymore, I overreacted, and she is moving out. She said it so calmly and emotionless you would have thought nothing happened. A week before the club altercation we had just renewed out apartment lease, to get ready for my 3L year. I did not see this coming at all. It was a knife wound to the back, how could she be so emotionless, so heartless, so nonchalant about this relationship that had been going on for three years?

After I got back to Montgomery I started to think about our relationship over the past few years. I started to think maybe I was a little responsible for her cheating. I thought it was my fault somehow. My fault that she felt lonely and had to seek companionship from another man. My fault for putting law school before her. My fault for not being a better boyfriend.

I had one more trick up my sleeve before I was going to call it quits for good. I was going to ask her to marry me when she got home. Earlier that day I went to the jewelry store and bought a very nice ring that I could not afford. When she got home I pulled the ring out of my pocket, got on one knee like how they do in the movies and asked.

She looked at it and said no. Well she did not say "no" directly, but she did not say yes. When asking a woman for her hand in marriage anything besides hysterical screaming and yelling is a no. She looked at me started crying and I just walked out. That was it. There was nothing left to say after that. Her job as a teacher at a local school was over the end of that week, she packed some of her clothes and left.

I eventually returned to the apartment saddened, confused and heart broken. Summer school was about to start in a few days. I did not have time to be heartbroken it was time to continue with school. The whole summer was terrible. I was heartbroken, I could not focus and I was not eating. I had numerous Sickle Cell Crises because I was so sad. Monica was not only my lover but my best friend, she had been with me throughout my entire law school career. I did not know how I was going to continue without her. It was funny, I used to see all my friends heart broken and laugh like man just go get another woman. But when someone that close betrays you in the most hurtful way, it is hard to forget it and replace them.

I finished the summer semester up and did well. That summer was the worst though. All the extra alone time I had on my hands was used wisely though with me taking courses over the summer. Monica eventually did come back to retrieve the rest of her stuff, she had moved in a neighborhood a few miles away from me and gotten into a relationship with little dude. This was the worst summer of my life. I buried myself in school work just so I would not feel hurt and have to face the reality of what happened. I did rather well that summer semester but even the good grades could not mend my broken heart. I felt betrayed, I felt used, and abandoned. I allowed Monica to move in with me during my first year of law school while she looked for worked and began her teaching career. She had begun her career and realized she did not need me anymore and I had to come to grips with it. That was it. She had her new man, new place, and I was all alone entering my last year of law school with a broken heart and chip on my shoulder.

# Chapter 18

## THIRD YEAR

After my 2L year which had ended with a bang to say the least. I spent the entire summer taking extra summer classes to ensure I graduated on time. Rachel, and Tiffany who had become my new law school best friends knew about everything. They stayed with me throughout it all checking on me and telling me it would be okay. Now, I am a third-year law student going to court, class and just adjusting to the bachelor life. I even had a few dates with a couple of the new incoming female law students. Things were looking up slowly, but surely.

About a month in to my 3L year I got a call from Monica. She said she wanted to talk. I ask "For what?" she says it was important. We met at a burger joint by the school. I walked in on the phone and her face lights up. I sat down very nonchalant before hanging up the phone. I looked over the menu and did not pay attention to her I asked "What would you like to talk about Monica? Does your boyfriend know you are here?" "I miss you" she said. While I was missing her like crazy too but I could not let her know. "I miss you too" I mumbled. She smiled. She then asks me how I had been. We engaged in small talk as we waited for the food to come out. She apologized for everything she had done said she regretted not taking the ring from the proposal. While I admit, it was nice to hear. But I told her I could not accept her apology. She asked "Why not?" I told her it was a kind gesture, but you disrespected me in public on social media in front of all our family and friends with the post you made after the club incident, therefore the only apology I am accepting will be a public one. She looked at me like I was crazy. I did not care though I am real big on respect you cannot embarrass someone in public and apologize to them in private. That is not a valid apology.

As we waited for the food, she opened up a little more about why she left and how she regretted it. However, the conversation took a turn when she mentioned how Little Dude had a full-time job, how he was about to go back to college, and how he recently gotten her some new hair weave, -like she was bragging. I looked up from eating my food and I must have had a look of disgust on face because she asked me, "What?" I said nothing. In my head, I am thinking she still does not even realize what she lost. I was going to buy her a house, give her a family, take care of her for the rest of our lives and she is bragging about a pack of hair weave that cost $89.99. It was clear that I had bigger dreams then Monica and although my loyalty wanted to see if this could still work. My common sense told me it was time to make her a thing of the past. I ate the rest of my burger, left a five-dollar bill on the table for the waiter headed to the exit and left her with the bill.

I included my love life specifically for Jordan. She is engaged and her fiancé is thinking about coming to live with her. This is a situation I have seen numerous times. Usually, when a spouse/significant other comes to live with the law student it ends in one of two ways. The first being that their bond is strong and the couple makes it through all three years of law school. The second and more common way is that it results in a break up. As I said before law school is like a mistress it takes a lot of your time up when done correctly. When a spouse moves with the law student it is just as hard on them as it is on you. The spouse will be in a brand-new city, no family, no job and no friends. This will be a big adjustment and on top of everything you will be gone most of the day and when you are home you will just want to sleep. Fortunately, for Jordan the relationships seem to have a better success rate when men come with their counterparts than when a woman comes with her counterpart to law school.

Law school will be a true test for their relationship especially since they will be newlyweds. I encourage her to sit down and talk with her fiancé. This decision will impact not only her life but his life severely. Law school is going to change her.

Unfortunately, the person who he marries this summer will not exactly be the same person a year or two from now. Go over who will handle the finances, will he be okay with the long study nights when you do not get home until late? These are the type of situations that will crumble marriages. She should have a talk with herself asking and ask is my fiancé more of a distraction when I learn or is he helpful? Is he the type of guy who will need a lot of constant attention? When I am mad does he calm me down or make me angrier? This is what she will have to look at. Her coming to law school will not only affect her life but also the people around her.

## Let's Go to Court

3L year is the year I am spending the most time in the courtroom. In the last year of law school, they issue third- year practice cards. This card allows one to practice law beside a real attorney under their supervision. I went back home to Georgia and started following Attorney Thomas. He is a nice attorney who is a sole practitioner in Columbus, Georgia. Attorney Thomas took me under his wing which I will always be grateful for and showed me some things that could not be taught in a law book. I ran into Mrs. King again a few weeks ago while in court. She said she remembered me, but I do not think she really did. Her mouth said she remembered me, but her face said I have never seen this kid a day before in my life. Ironically, I will never forget her or her Criminal Law Class in college as it was one of the first times I found my love for the law.

It was hard to believe that I had been gone for three years and I was finally back home interacting with people who I admired growing up. I met Attorney Jackson, he is the most known Criminal Defense Attorney in the city of Columbus. To my surprise, he had already heard about me before we officially met. Another attorney who stuck out to me was Attorney Kendrick I met him during a court proceeding. He is another well-known criminal defense attorney and he has locs as well. Now when I return to Columbus and start practicing law I will not be the first lawyer there with locs, I thought that was cool and interesting. It is good to know I will not have to go through the constant staring and stereotypes I went through 1L year.

## Back to Business

In my 3L year, my popularity has risen tremendously throughout the school. Not to brag but I am the man here. I am a class favorite and probably the most well-known student on campus. I remember like a month or two ago my professor stopped me in the hallway and told me that he had a review session and a girl asked for the outlines from the previous class and he told her to get the outline from Ralston. He said she replied "Who is Ralston?" and the whole classroom went silent. He said he replied, "Where are you from Mars? Everyone knows Ralston" and we laughed. But people knew me that is why he would give the outlines to me first because he knew everyone knew who I was and I was not a hard person to find on a campus like Faulkner. I was always a jokester and I have a vibrant personality. Some of the nicest things I have ever heard here was when someone said they "like to sit by me because I always give off good vibes and energy" or another classmate said "I was probably the nicest person he had met while at law school." But, quite frankly I was doing nothing but treating people how I wanted them to treat me when I first came here.

Another reason I have become so well liked is because there was not a lot to do in Montgomery so I often host parties at my home Friday nights. The parties are great. I had a bachelor's pad after Monica had moved out and would often stay in the big apartment by myself. The gatherings started out of boredom, I was at school one day and thought to invite people over Friday night. A great friend of mine named Betsi who is a petite white woman with a big southern accent and a vibrant personality similar to mine became friends with me our 3L year. We were so opposite but so alike when it came to our joyful personalities. A few days before the get together, Betsi says "Hey, Ralston can't wait to come to your hang-back. Do you need me to bring anything?" I look confusingly at her and say "the what Betsi?" she says "the hang-back, the party at your house Friday" I say "Betsi it's called a kick back". She looked at me in disbelief and says "oh my gosh, I've been calling it a hang back this entire time I've told my mother, and brother about how the cool kids call a party a hang back now." We both started laughing hysterically. But that was one of the things I liked most about law school, the mixing of cultures. I was from west Georgia and a kickback to me was a usual word to describe a small gathering of friends. But Betsi is from a small town in Northern Alabama and had never heard of the slang term. Eventually, the word spread and I started inviting the entire school to my kickbacks or "Hang Backs" as Betsi were telling them. With my vibrant personality, and the boredom the small city of Montgomery often bought I was not surprised by the number of people who would show up. I do not drink but my apartment would be full of beer, liquor and wine for the guests. Not to mention I would always cook plenty of food for everyone to show off my culinary skills. Beer pong, rap music, spades, and great people; law school was starting to look up. These people were my friends, maybe more than friends, we had laughed together, cried together, been confused and scared together ever since 1L year.

## Smooth Operator

While I had lost my best friend, I did develop a stronger relationship with my peers during my 3L year. Eventually, I start dating again. My friends back home told me about online dating and I tried that for a while. Law school bought me popularity and power with that comes the women. It was unbelievable how after my relationship they came fast almost as if they were waiting for me to get out of my relationship. Between the women back home who found out I was newly single, the women I would meet around Montgomery and the ones from online dating I always had company. When women see a nice guy, with no kids and in law school a-lot will not reject you. Some did, but most did not.

The craziest thing that happen to me since I have been single occurred about two weeks ago. I was leaving court dressed up and headed to class. Being in court all morning I was hungry and I stopped at a fast food restaurant. The girl at the window took my name from my debit card and found me on social media to ask me for my number. I was not sure if I should be flattered or to call the police. I have had women from Columbus come to Montgomery, about a 90-minute drive, from Atlanta about a 120-minute drive and even Florida about a 180-minute drive. The furthest visitor to come was from California she got on a plane and flew out simply because I asked her to. I realized I had to slow down when I accidentally had three dates in one day. I took one girl to breakfast; another girl took me to lunch and the last one was supposed to come over and hang out but we end up going to the movies so three in one day. The truth is though all those women I had and I still felt lonely inside because it was not the person I really wanted to be with. It was fun though and I guess I should clear up that I did not sleep with all of them, sometimes I would just like company around so I would not be in the apartment alone. The bachelor life was okay I met some nice women, but it is too expensive and time consuming. On top of that it was taking my focus off school which I could not let happen. The main objective coming here was to focus on school, therefore I was determined not to let the recent change of events distract me from graduating.

## Seeking Help

My last semester in law school had arrived. My grades were good, I had money in my pocket and more women after me than I had ever dreamed of, but I still found myself not being truly happy anymore. I noticed I kept getting crises a little more than usual just from every day typical stress. On the advice of a friend, I decided to go and see the school therapist. At first I objected, like a therapist? I am not crazy, I just have a broken heart. I fought a little while but eventually I gave in; it was hard though. I was Mr. Big Shot, the funny man, the one who everyone comes to see when they have problems I did not need therapy. I am the professional problem solver. I do not get advice from others on my problems, or so I thought. But I eventually did go.

Therapy, is one of the best things I have ever done. In the Black community, therapy is not utilized. As a man, a Black man especially, we are supposed to suck stuff up and show no emotion. As a future lawyer now, I recommend therapy for everyone. I enjoyed therapy because it was a chance to talk to a neutral party, who would not judge me. I could not talk to my parents about the depression I was feeling, they would have worried themselves to death. I could not talk to my sister about it, knowing her she would try to beat Monica up or something. Therapy was my release.

As a 3L, I was actually meeting with clients and giving legal advice to them under the supervision of a licensed attorney. I was listening to people's problems all the time, therapy was the only time I got to express my problems to anyone. My therapist is the one who informed me I had never really healed from my relationship. I just submerged myself in work to forget about the hurt I was feeling on the inside and that this probably played a part in why I was feeling terrible. Mental health is just as important as physical health. Law school is a very stressful place and with my health conditions I could not afford to take a chance of getting sick during my last semester and missing too many days. Eventually, my therapist and I became friends I would give him advice sometimes just as he would me. As I continued to go, the crises slowed down, I felt better over time and eventually started feeling like my normal self again. I had gotten my physical health under control. Attending therapy was my release of stress and allowed for me to have a healthy mental state which is an essential part in my fight with Sickle Cell.

I recommend the school's therapist for both Jordan and Nicholas. Therapy was very therapeutic to say the least. The only regret I have is not going sooner. When I first got to law school I was an outcast. I was different and I did not fit in. I acted like it did not bother me, but it did. After I had gotten sick before finals and watched people who I knew I was smarter than excel while I had to deal with this chronic illness and still keep a smile on face the entire time. I acted like it did not bother me, but it did. Then the constant battle to try to prove myself, the constant hospitalizations, getting yelled at by faculty members. I just let everything roll off my shoulders and kept pushing. Finally, after being betrayed by the person I was sleeping in bed with every night for the past three years and just shrugging it off like it had not happened. It was simply too much to handle. When you let problems build up without really dealing with them, eventually they will deal with you. Therapy was cool and I recommend Jordan going to therapy because there will be problems within her marriage eventually. For Nicholas, I recommend therapy because sometimes having Sickle Cell can get very stressful and too much stress for a person with Sickle Cell and it will take a toll on your body. On top of this you are a young Black male. Contrary to popular belief, we have emotions and we tend to not show them as much as we probably should. But sometimes we need to show our emotions, it gets rough for us especially in this line of work.

## Sickle Cell & Law School

I am currently composing my Rigorous Writing Paper. A Rigorous Writing Paper is similar to a Dissertation a doctor would do upon leaving medical school. Our professor asked us all if there was one law we could change what would it be? I chose to write my paper about the federal prohibition of marijuana. It took hours on top of hours of legal researching in order for my paper to be an intelligent, well written document. While my classmates still do not know about my constant fight with Sickle Cell they assumed I was a pothead, (I baked them brownies to eat while I did an oral presentation on my paper, the professor even jokingly asked did they contain pot) we all laughed after I told them, "No, they are not cannabis edibles." I ultimately am writing this paper for a different, more serious reason then they understand. The reasoning for the paper explained the injustices of the ban and most importantly the medical contribution cannabis provides.

While I will not elaborate too much on it because I am still currently writing the paper. I go into vivid detail about the injustices the federal ban on marijuana has caused to many minority classes, specifically younger Hispanic and African Americans males. I then elaborate on the discriminatory background of the prohibition and take a stance by attacking Harry Anslinger the man responsible for the ban who was a known racist. After elaborating why the ban should have never been implemented in the first place, I then take a legal stance point and discuss the benefits the United States would derive from the removal of the ban.

The pain from my Sickle Cell is a daily battle. I consistently take many pills. Studies have shown marijuana is of great use to Sickle Cell patients and other patients of chronic illnesses who are in constant pain. This will be the only time I would even remotely talk about Sickle Cell in law school (besides this memorandum). It was kind of cool though incorporating Sickle Cell and law school. The paper is entitled Remove the Ban: A Legal Analysis Calling For the Removal of the Federal Ban From the Ideologies of John Locke, Thomas Aquinas, and Jeremey Bentham.

## Heading Home

I am currently enrolled in the Elder Law Clinic. The Elder Law Clinic is a free program that Faulkner offers to the local citizens who need legal services. I enjoy working with the elderly and the local citizens of Montgomery are always very friendly. For the first time, I feel like I am making a difference. I am drafting and executing wills like a real attorney.

The Elder Law Clinic is great. We make a big difference in the community. I had a client fall on campus as she left our meeting and a client of the clinic die recently; I am not sure how I feel about elder law anymore. The client I had who fell reminded me of my grandmother who passed away a few years prior to me coming to law school. We had an initial meeting and everything went well I watched her walk back to her car and when she was almost there I went back inside. Several moments go by and one of the professors comes back in the room with my client and says he found her in the parking lot on the ground. I instantly felt horrible, while I had watched her walk to the car, I felt bad I did not make sure she got in the car. I asked her what happened and she said she fell over after the wind had blew her papers away and she reached down to get them and lost her balance. I felt terrible for a few weeks and even now I get sad thinking about it. Law school is more than just reading and writing, towards the end I am starting to see that people's lives are in my hands. While she told me not to worry about it, I still walk her to her car now. She is getting better and her wounds are healing. I do not know if I will continue to do elder law when I start practicing in Georgia, but the Elder Law Clinic Faulkner provides is definitely helpful overall.

## Was it Worth it?

Was law school worth the hassle? I do not know if right now is the perfect time for me to answer that question for Jordan. I may have to update this memorandum in a year or two after graduation and taking the bar. I am not sure if the degree is worth the blood, sweat, and tears I have put in to it. But what I do know is that when applying for jobs I will stand out. Employers will have 100 resumes on their desk, but what is going to make my resume stand out is my law degree.

Law school is not an easy decision to make. Talk to your family, think on it and make the best decision for yourself. It is a hard task, but achievable with the right amount of dedication. The number one excuse I hear from people who are thinking about law school is "I'm not ready." I usually reply with "Who is?" No one has ever made history playing it safe. Someone told me one time if you are waiting for your life to be completely in order before you make your next move, then good luck with that. When I went off to law school I was poor. I mean very poor like down to my last few hundreds of dollars and in a relationship, but I just had to pick up what I had and make a run for it. If I had waited to get married or to be financially stable, then I may have never come. Law school is an opportunity -nothing more nothing less. You can either be the girl who went to law school or the girl twenty years from now in a job she hates wondering what her life would have been like had she went to law school.

I think Jordan is just nervous, as she should be. Law school can be a scary place. My advice to her would be to attend if accepted. If her passion is to be an adoption lawyer, then this is the right place for her. Do not worry about all of the finances and the things that could possibly go wrong while she is here, just focus on the long-term goal of passing the bar, becoming a lawyer and getting her first adoption completed. To ask if law school was worth the money or the pain and suffering would require a subjective answer; some people will say it was, while others will say it is not. She is the one of the top students at her college and if this is her passion she would be doing herself a disservice if she decided not to come due to the cost. I come from a middle-class upbringing. While I am in debt now, Faulkner has provided me with a great scholarship to help me pay for law school. I often tell myself the moment I win my first big case it will all be worth it.

As, I wrap up this memorandum, I just want to emphasize that law school just like life is only enjoyable for me if I am helping other people out. My start at Jones was rocky, but by staying true to myself and being a genuine person, people eventually gravitated towards me. Law school is tough, but completing law school while suffering from a chronic illness is very tough. But, if I can do it, so can Jordan, Nicholas and others. My journey has taught me that law school is a marathon. There may be detours. Sometimes you will have to stop and get water. Other times you may have to stop and change your shoes, but the main thing is to keep running. Whether you come in first place or last place you have completed the race and you should be proud of yourself. These next couple of weeks before my graduation will come and go and I plan to enjoy them.

# Conclusion

In conclusion, this memorandum will be of great use to the advisement of Jordan and Nicholas both before they come to law school and even while they are in law school. I have covered everything of importance and even added things that they did not specifically inquire about, but I think will helpful for them to know. Law school is a journey one must complete for themselves. While I hope, they do take heed and listen so they do not make the same mistakes as I have made, the determinate of success will be ultimately upon them.

April 28, 2017 (Two weeks before graduation)

(Knock on door)

**Me:** Dean Rivera?

**Dean Rivera:** Hey, Mr. Jarrett. I received your memorandum.

**Me:** Oh, did you? How did you like it? I hope I did not get too personal.

**Dean Rivera:** No Mr. Jarrett, it was great. I am thinking about even letting all the incoming students read it for themselves since you incorporated so much valuable information. I know it was originally supposed to only be for Jordan and Nicholas but do you think it would be okay to advise other students as well with it.

**Me:** (I smile) Yes, that is fine. Hey as long as I get my credits to graduate you may do whatever you please with it.

**Dean Rivera:** Why thank you Mr. Jarrett and as promised you will graduate. I am sorry we did not catch the mishap earlier, but I am glad you were able to share your story with us. The memorandum gave the staff and I a lot of insight on the school.

**Me:** You let the entire staff read it? Man, I hope I did not get anyone in trouble.

**Dean Rivera**: No, actually quite the opposite. Being part of the faculty myself not only was it helpful in the advising of Jordan and Nicholas but to myself as well. The memorandum gave us a good look at our program from an outside view. All of the administration here consists of seasoned attorney's, we often forget the struggles that come with law school and this was just a wake-up call for all of us. So, thank you the writing was clear, concise and very informative. The story telling was brilliant. While I was reading it I would sometimes close my eyes and imagine that I was actually there with you. We plan to do some improvements especially with regard to the attendance policy for students with special needs and I just want you know I am personally proud of you. I was proud before, but after reading the memorandum I have a new found respect for you Mr. Jarrett.

**Me**: Aww shucks Dean Rivera, you are going to make my eyes start to water.

**Dean Rivera**: (She smiles) Are you ready for graduation?

**Me**: No, but I will be.

**Dean Rivera**: Why not?

**Me**: I am not sure. It is something I always wanted, but now that is has arrived I am not sure how to feel.

**Dean Rivera**: I think that is just the jitters talking. If there is any student in the school who is ready to get out there and impact the world with the skills they have learned at Faulkner it is you Mr. Jarrett. I have watched you for the last three years not only become a great student , but a great person and I am pleased to have the privilege of saying that you are a part of our school's history.

**Me**: Well thank you Dean Rivera. I really do appreciate your kind and encouraging words.

**Dean Rivera**: No problem. Is there anything else?

**Me**: No ma'am.

**Dean Rivera:** Alright Mr. Jarrett, you are all cleared for graduation and I will you see May 13th.

**Me**: Thank you.

# The End

# EPILOGUE

# To my fellow warriors:

To those with Sickle Cell I encourage you to live a long prosperous life just as if you did not have Sickle Cell. There will be good days and bad days. The best advice I can give is to find a routine. My crises usually occur when I am doing something out of my regular routine. Find a routine, stick with it and try not to deviate from it. If you wake up at 9:00am every day, wake up at 9:00am. If you work from 9:00am to 5:00pm, then continue to do so. Do not work 12 hour shifts your body is not used to. If on a crisis free day, you drink a gallon of water and no Crisis occurred then continue to drink a gallon of water every day.

Unfortunately, you may have to abstain from some activities for health reasons. There will be somethings your mind wants to do but your body simply cannot. I tried to play basketball recently to relieve my stress, halfway through the game I had a crisis and stopped playing. Sickle Cell does not control you but, somethings you enjoy you may have to give up. Mine happen to be basketball.

Watch your diet. One's diet plays a big part in staying healthy especially for us. I find myself eating home cooked food, drinking less soda, plenty of Gatorade and water. Having Sickle Cell is one of the reasons I became such a good chef. I would cook sometimes when my parents had to work late. I really started cooking when I moved away from home and I did not have access to my mother's cooking. Fast food was convenient, but was making me sick, so I taught myself how to cook.

Find a good doctor. I never liked going to doctors, hematologists or specialists due to the fact that I felt that they placed all Sickle Cell patients in the same category. Many doctors have a pre-conceived notion in their head that Sickle Cell patients are pain medication abusers. Most doctors I come in to contact with ask me the same questions repeatedly. When were, you diagnosed? How often do you have a crisis? Then proceed to tell me how to live my life while giving me little to no pain medicine. They would always try to throw the few FDA approved drugs they had for Sickle Cell on to me and persuade me how it was so good for me. I tried them for a while but did not feel much of a difference. So I eventually stopped taking them and stop going to the doctor. But now since law school is wrapping up I will find a doctor who has experience with Sickle Cell patients upon my return to Georgia. As time progresses the things that your body cannot do will become apparent. I wish it was something I could say or do to minimize the number or completely stop anybody from ever suffering from a Sickle Cell Crisis again. The truth is every Sickle Cell patient is different and we all have certain things that will trigger a Sickle Cell Crisis in a matter of minutes. My advice is to find those triggers and do anything possible to prevent them from reoccurring. Wisdom comes with age and you will eventually figure out how to minimize the pain and number of crises.

I almost ended up having to drop out of law school because I was missing too many days and not adhering to the attendance policy due to being sick. After a crisis, it would take a full day to recover to normal. I would have them at night usually, about three in the morning and I would not feel good the rest of the day. I would not eat anything, did not want to move, and definitely did not want to attend class.

One thing I learned about myself while attending law school is that when my body hurts from a Sickle Cell Crisis I do not learn well. When I am in physical pain it throws my whole mental state into a disarray. As time went on I started to see that in order for me to be completely attentive; I could not be in pain. Now there were plenty of days I went to class while in the midst of having a Sickle Cell Crisis and heavily medicated on pain pills (Percocet to be exact). I would go to class and act like nothing was wrong. I was there physically, but mentally I would be hoping and praying for the pain to go away so I could attentively focus and not fall behind. My main objective was to not let Sickle Cell hinder my dreams. Do you know a doctor once told me that I should not work? He said I should live the most stress-free life as possible and avoid anything that could potentially affect my Sickle Cell. I never returned to see him again. It was devastating, I felt as if he was telling me I could not be anything because of this disease. That is the exact opposite of what I want people to take from this book. The sky is really the limit. If you do not have Sickle Cell or a chronic illness this should encourage you because I have a bigger struggle than you, so what is your excuse that is stopping you from being great? If you are diagnosed with Sickle Cell this should encourage you to strive for more because we are fighting the same battle and I made it. Therefore, you can as well. There were plenty of days especially, in the winter, when my legs would be hurting very bad because of the temperature outside. But I just kept pushing. Sickle Cell became a game to me, it was an experiment. I would get a crisis and then think about what I was doing when that happen in order to avoid it the next time. If I would be eating food, then I would not eat that food again, if I went to a place that was too hot or too cold then I would not go there again. Eventually it sort of became a game to see if I could reduce the number of Sickle Cell Crises I had per year.

I remember being in so much pain at times that I stopped believing in God. I could not imagine what kind of God would let me endure this amount of pain. It is very hard to have faith, when hurting both mentally and physically. The important thing though is to never give up and keep pushing. The worst thing to do is to let this disease have too much power over you.

Keep your head up and always keep a positive attitude. People look up to us (believe it or not) because of how strong we are. Even if the doctors think we are exaggerating pain levels in order to obtain medicine. The truth is a doctor can only sympathize and can never feel the amount of pain a person with Sickle Cell endures.

If you are a family member of someone with Sickle Cell the best advice I can give is just to be there for them. Do not go around feeling sorry for them and treating them differently. Just be there, the worst thing you could do is to leave someone alone because you figured they probably did not want to be bothered. Go to the hospital, bring a balloon, flowers, food, whatever to just let them know you are thinking about them. That helps a lot for me, especially when I am not feeling good. The hospital is a depressing place and it is always good to be surrounded by the people you love when you have to go through hard times.

Money plays a big part in health. Unfortunately, many Sickle Cell Warriors do not have the funds to live the lifestyle they need to keep them healthy. Everyone does not have insurance. For those people who do, insurance my not cover the total cost of all doctor or emergency room visits. On top of that it's hard to find and keep employment when you have Sickle Cell with the long periods of recovery after a Sickle Cell Crisis many jobs will not allow for this. Fortunately, I did have insurance. But the food I had to buy to stay healthy often got expensive and my medications can be costly as well.

I often invest in things that help me prevent the crisis before it even begins. I got a remote control start on my car so the car would be running with heat circulating by the time I got in. In Montgomery, I got an apartment with a garage attached to it. Those cold mornings did not make me feel so bad anymore. This helped a lot, cold weather was always a trigger of mine and often the start of a Sickle Cell Crisis. I would go to my car in the garage, arrive to the school, park in the handicap parking spot closest to the school, and run in the building. It is little things like this that ultimately help and are worth the extra expenses. The remote start was a couple of hundred dollars and the first level apartment with an attached garage was an extra one hundred and fifty dollars a month on top of my rent. It reduced the number of Crises, I had so I say it was money well spent.

I always say Sickle Cell saved my life while killing me at the same time. I have had some very life changing moments during a Sickle Cell Crisis. I do not know if it was me being under the influence of the pain medication or what, but one day I woke up with the mindset that I will not let this defeat me. The truth is I do not know how long I have to live so, therefore, I am going to make the best out of every day while I can. For motivation on days I want to give up I listen to Prodigy who is also a Sickle Cell survivor. Boosie is another rapper I like. He is a diabetic, he has many motivational songs about how he has gotten through his medical struggles. The rapper Future has a sister that has Sickle Cell, so I have taken a liking to him. I listen to a lot of Future, especially when not feeling well. These are things I do to get through my Sickle Cell Crises and I hope my sharing of them will help others through their times of distress. So, until a cure is found we all will just have to keep our heads up and take it one day at a time. And remember STAY HYDRATED!!!

# To my future lawyers:

Before applying to law school just reflect on this book. Think about everything I mentioned and do the balancing test I gave. My law degree will make me an elite job candidate. While that is the good thing do not forget all of the bad things that came with getting it too. I lost a few friends to jealousy, I lost my girlfriend, I will wear glasses for the rest of my life, I now suffer from insomnia because my mind is always working. I think differently, I speak differently, I over analyze things that probably do not need to be over analyzed.

Law school really does change you in ways you cannot imagine. Some of the things you enjoyed before law school will not excite you anymore. I remember before I left for school I would love to go out to the local night club. Now I do not enjoy it as much. I went to one recently and was dissatisfied. While it was good to see old friends, I begin to notice that some people do this every week. They go to work Monday through Friday just to go out on Friday nights. Not saying I am better than anyone, but I do not enjoy it anymore. What exactly am I celebrating? A party for me means celebrating. Usually after an accomplishment or special event such as a birthday or promotion not a weekly event.

Nowadays I find myself studying at the nightclub. I am there physically, but mentally I am somewhere else thinking about the Federal Rules of Civil Procedure. Towards the end of law school while I was writing my rig and this book I would be in there, but I would be thinking about the paper I had to write when I got home, or thinking how I could be getting work done if I had not come out tonight.

Recently, I have been dragged out by friends who are proud of me getting ready to graduate and I have been out getting congratulated by people, but the whole time I am in there thinking I need to be home pre-studying for the bar. Also, you will feel yourself growing apart from close friends. A good friend of mine Kevan had abruptly stop speaking to me and we had not spoken to each other in two years since I left for

Montgomery. Eventually I found out he was kind of sad that I was moving away, but he came back around that's what real friends do. Now we talk like nothing has ever happened.

As far as friends go you will outgrow some. That is inevitable. Things you guys used to talk about all the time just will not seem interesting to you anymore. For me personally I must have balance between my law school friends and my hometown friends. I like talking to my law school friends because they understand the struggle of law school. They know of about the unsure feeling that causes knots in your stomach after taking a law school exam. But, my friends back home have known me since I have been a child and we can talk about things that happened 10 years ago that I cannot talk with my law school friends about.

This will tell you what goes on behind the scenes of law school. The pamphlet they give you when considering law school is not real. Do not be fooled by the smiling faces on the front of the brochure with attractive people smiling and having a good time like law school some sort of happy sanctuary. I see now that law schools will usually have three or four people typically two white men, and two white women. They will then place a few minorities in the picture usually, Asian, Indian and African American. I love the concept and how people are starting to recognize us, but do not let this fool you. In law school, there is still racism and still classifications of rich and poor. We do not all get along sometimes and some days you are going to even wonder why you decided to come.

Law school will eventually teach you things you did not know about yourself. Everything anyone has ever told you about law school FORGET IT. It does not matter if your dad, mom, uncle, sister, brother or whoever went and told you what to do. There is no right answer on how to make it in law school. Everyone must find out for themselves, what works for one may not work for another. I learned that I am more productive at night time, while a friend of mine works better in the morning. I learn the best by reading the material before bed and again first thing in the morning when waking up as this helps improve my memorization on the subject. There are a variety of ways to achieve success in law school you just have to find what works for you. There are no right or wrong ways to learn in law school. You will see visual learners and audio learners, the notecards and the poster board learners, and the laptop note takers and the hand-written note takers. These learning techniques will follow you throughout law school and will be very useful while studying for the bar.

Keep pushing, things will get better! This is the advice you will need in law school and life. If it were easy, everyone would be doing it. Find some motivation. I like Judge Mathis, he is a hero to me who I looked at, for motivation most days. I would often watch his show just to remind me that this mission was achievable. He was a man who came from the streets and now he is a judge. Judge Mathis motivated me to keep working hard and reminded me that you do not have to come from a family filled with lawyers and that you can know the streets and still have respect for the law.

I would also use my family for motivation often. I had a picture of them in my apartment that I would look at every morning. I always thought about my future kids as well when I wanted to quit. How could I tell them not to quit, if I had quit? I wanted them to be proud of their dad. Law school is like riding a bike, if you fall get back up. Look at my story, I almost got kicked out after my first semester, I have had numerous hospital visits due to my Sickle Cell, I have lost family members, I went through a heartbreak, I have been stereotyped, and discriminated against. But I never gave up. Every time a hurdle came, I found a way to overcome it. This type of determination is exactly what is needed. I wish I could tell you everything was fine and law school was not that bad. But the truth is law school is bad, law school is very bad at times. But what makes the difference between a law school graduate and a law school dropout is drive, work ethic, and ability to bounce back when life gets rough.

I am a smart guy, but there are law students who have done better than me. One can be the smartest person in the world, but if he does not work hard to strengthen his gift, someone can and will out work him. Law school went from being part of my life to my entire life. There was never a time I would be doing absolutely nothing, there is always some work to be done while in law school. If I wasn't doing anything pertaining to law school my conscience would make me feel guilty for not studying. Studying was like a drug, I did not feel right if I was not doing it. I tried watching TV one day while I was on Academic Probation, my conscience would not allow it. I needed to be watching a lecture video, updating my outline or reading for the next class. Unfortunately, there can only be one top scholar in the class and more than likely it will not be you. But if you put in the constant work and stay on top of things then the number you come in at the end of the marathon does not matter as long as you finish.

## What's next for Ralston?

The hardest thing about getting ready to graduate is the uncertainty. After I graduate in a few weeks then what? Will I pass the bar? The Georgia Bar is a two day, twelve-hour exam and after I graduate I will have nine weeks to prepare for it. What if I graduate law school, but become one of those people who cannot pass the bar? Or what if I pass the bar, but cannot seem to obtain a job? Will I stay and practice law in Georgia my entire career? As far as my personal life goes will I ever find love again? Will I ever get the little boy and twin girls that I wanted so bad? Will I ever get married? If I do get married one day will she like me for me or like me because I will be a successful attorney? Do I ask my wife for a prenuptial agreement? Or maybe I will marry another attorney. Will we have enough time for each other if both of us have demanding jobs? Will our egos get in the way and ruin our marriage? Will we be able to separate our occupations from our everyday lives? I do not know how fun life would be if my wife and I were cross examining each other at the dinner table every night about who was supposed to cook dinner or who was supposed to pick the kids up from school. It would go like this "You got off at 4:30pm correct?" "Yes." "Today is Wednesday, is that, not right?" "Yes," "Is it not true that you are designated to pick the kids up every Monday and Wednesday at 4:45pm?" I am just being funny, but I really do think about things like these.

Will I ever pay these student loans back? Will a client ever get mad at me and try to hurt my family and I? How long will I be able to practice law with Sickle Cell affecting my body daily? These are some of the many questions I ask myself. How I handle it is by not worrying too much about it. Whatever shall be, shall be. If I worried myself about what could happen, then I would not be focusing on the now which is the most important. Many people have been congratulating me because they know I am about to graduate law school. I on the other hand am just trying to remain as humble as I can. While I am about to graduate and I am proud of myself, I am very uncertain what the future will hold for me. But I will continue to take it one day at a time and let the chips fall where they may.

# Letter to my Fallen Warriors

Dear Prodigy,

Hey man. I'm damn near in tears writing this. When I heard about your death I was studying at my kitchen table, took a break for a second and logged into social media. I saw the rest in peace posts but I still did not believe it at first. Then Havoc confirmed it. Although we never met, I don't think anyone knows how much I looked up to you when it comes to this Sickle Cell shit. "You could never feel my pain" was more than a song, it was an anthem for me. I remember "Shook ones" came out I couldn't be any more than five or six and my pops told me that you had Sickle Cell the same disease as me. Although I knew nothing about it at the time, I thought you were the coolest dude on the planet. As I got older I remember watching your YouTube videos for hours just listening to your interviews about how you take care of yourself. Hell, I remember even turning my radio off a few times while listening to Tupac's "Hit em up" because he dissed you at the end when he made the comment about Sickle Cell. You were more than just a rapper to me. Who am I supposed to look up to now that you are gone? Who is going to be the new leader of this Sickle Cell movement that we so desperately need? I am not sure if I can handle all of that. Well I know you are probably busy up there but I just wanted to talk to you for a second. May God rest your soul.

Your number one fan,

Ralston Jarrett, J.D.

Dear Michael,

Man it wasn't supposed to end like this. You came to law school after I had already graduated but as always, I made it my business to know everyone on campus especially the Black men. I remember our first encounter while a very brief encounter I will never forget it. I was studying to take the bar and my little bro Shevon called me and said that the last final for first semester was over tomorrow. I took the day off from studying and drove from Columbus to Montgomery to have lunch with not only him, but all of the young Black law students. I pulled up and I saw you over there, I immediately recognize you and Ashley from Facebook. We all talked and I told you guys not to worry about grades as they are out of your hands now, then we went to Applebee's. I am talking to you guys as we wait on our food and I asked you a question. You looked at me and responded but I cannot help to notice the yellowish tint in your eyes. I want to ask you if you have Sickle Cell at this moment, but I hold my tongue as it was not the right time. The food comes, we ate, I tell you guys how proud I am of you all and I head home. Five weeks later, while I was studying in the library I received the news you were gone. I felt terrible I wanted to talk to you about managing this disease and law school at the same time unfortunately I was so consumed with studying for the bar, I never got the chance. I am proud of you though. You did a full semester of law school while battling Sickle Cell. That is an accomplishment. I do not care what Faulkner or anyone else says you will always be the second law student in our school's history to graduate from Jones with Sickle Cell Disease and my brother for life. May God rest your soul. Until we meet again.

Your brother for life,

Ralston Jarrett, J.D

# ABOUT THE AUTHOR

**Ralston Jarrett** was born with Sickle Cell Disease. Despite many health issues he started attending college at the early age of 17, where he majored in Criminal Justice. After college he attended law school with plans of becoming a criminal defense attorney and has recently graduated receiving his Juris Doctor degree. He now lives in Georgia and is currently preparing to sit for the upcoming Georgia Bar Examination.

**For more information visit:**

Instagram Mr_Challenger_
Twitter: InMyNinetyFives
Facebook: Ralston Jarrett

Made in the USA
Middletown, DE
22 June 2018